THE SCOWL

IRONSCYTHE SAGAS:

K.J. HERITAGE

SYGASM

FOR 'TWO-GUN BOB'

Contents

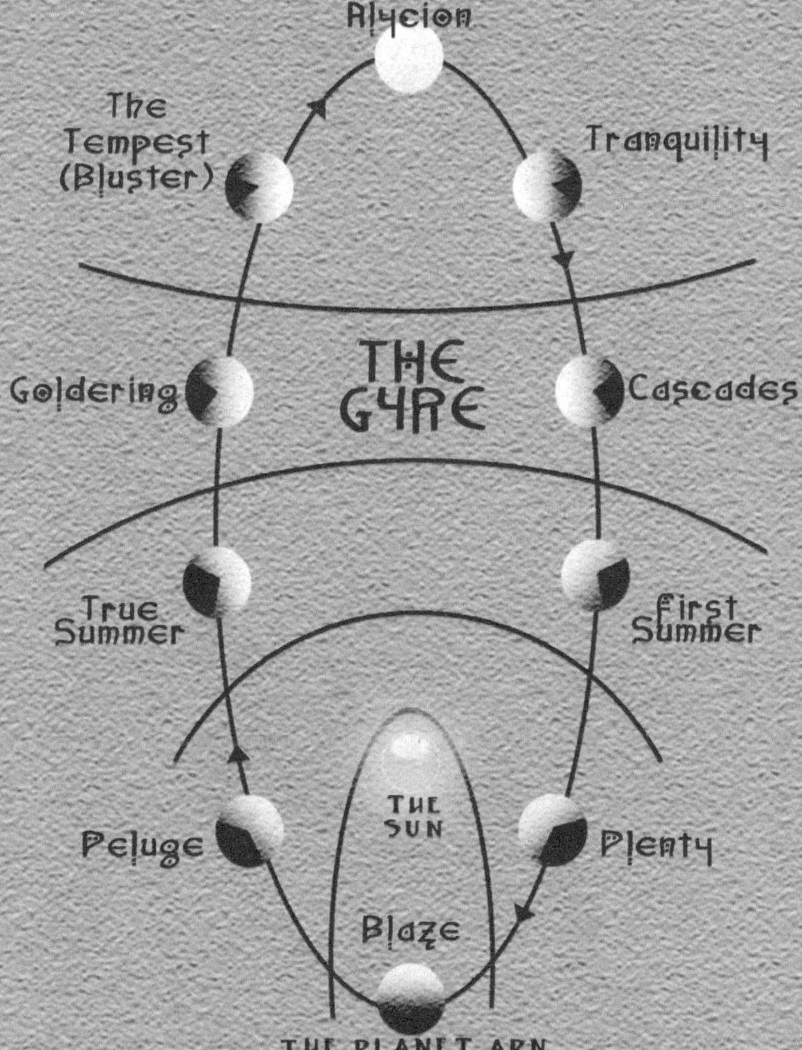

SEASONS OF ARN
ELTIRREN (COLDSTAR)
Alycion
The Tempest (Bluster)
Tranquility
THE GYRE
Goldering
Cascades
True Summer
First Summer
Peluge
THE SUN
Plenty
Blaze
THE PLANET ARN

N
THE MOST NORTHWEST POINT OF ARN
CARR
The Carline
OLDIVA
The Salted Wastes
ARIVA
Fangarra
Aiden
Keep Krall
Dol
Jorn

Jamlk
Starr
Murkhaven
Pelving Mines
Hollow Marshes
The Grikes
Fisk
PALIMARA
Palim
The Forest Hinterlan of Calbian
Krag
Morish
Riorta
The Gundrun Sea
TRI
KING
ONE
sk
HE
DDEN
LS

THE SCOWL: PART ONE

FLESH GOLEM

And from the dark unknown came a hooded avenger, a sable-weaved nemesis branded with living iron whose will it was to destroy all works of delving. His name? He had many over the great swathe of his lifetime, but history remembers him only as… Scowl.

The IronScythe Sagas, Cairn.

WEREGILD

WITH AN irritated flurry, King-Emperor Jhaz'Elrad and his entourage burst into the Reeving Chamber—a vast, lop-sided cauldron of a room with a vaulted ceiling and high open windows. The space, like all others in Castle Fangarra, was built from thin blocks of soot-coloured shale rudely cemented together and smoothed into swirls of black and white striating lines. A coarse wind blew steadily, groaning like a dying child, turning wall-mounted cressets red, their embers glowing and smoking. A pale imitation of the King-Emperor's own plush quarters.

Fools and idiots! This place stinks of them, thought Jhaz'Elrad, pulling his rich furs close against the cold and nodding towards his perfumers. *The Archon has gone too far this time. I am not some vassal at his disposal. I am King!*

A crowd waited in the dimness, but they did not notice the entrance of their liege. The King-Emperor was about to rectify that with an indignant shout, but stopped in his tracks. A monster lay in the centre of the chamber. An ugly naked pile of distorted, twisted limbs, staked to the floor under a net of ropes. The creature moaned unintelligibly, its voice blending with the wind. Keening. Lost. Hands, darting like hunting spiders, lurched from the abnormal body and scrabbled at the uneven paving stones.

The king did a double take. *Is it a man?*

"Make way for his eminence, King-Emperor Jhaz'Elrad!"

The crowd parted, some tripping over their own feet to get out of the way of the rapidly approaching entourage. Jhaz'Elrad strode forward onto a raised dais of carved, filigreed stone and ascended his throne.

Archon Glave—a rotund, self-satisfied tub of a man with an appetite for politics that outshone his liege—bowed. "Your Eminence."

For a second, Jhaz'Elrad entertained the notion of kicking the man in his fat backside, but thought better of it. "You dare to summon me," he whispered. "You go too far."

Glave straightened, his plump hands coming together in a fleshy union atop his immense belly, a half-apologetic smile plastered across his face. A single wart squatted in the crease of his nose like a red berry. "Forgive me, Eminence, if I took you away from any… important matters of state," he said with the barest flick of his eyebrows, "but a situation has arisen requiring your presence." He nodded towards the foul creature and grimaced.

"Do not push your King-Emperor too far, Archon. You overstep your mark." Jhaz'Elrad paused. The Archon was the kingdom's magistrate, his direct representative who dealt with petty squabbles and disputes. A small man with a lot of power. He tapped his sceptre, a rod of black fenneral (the hardest and most expensive of all stones) against the Archon's bulbous chest. Both men knew the significance of the gesture. One word from the king and Glave's life would be forfeit.

His smile did not waver. "I apologise most humbly, oh wise one."

The king sat back and shrugged. *The Archon knows his worth. But no one is indispensable.* "You better have a good explanation for interrupting my private recreations."

"A fool young noble of the court has been murdered."

"As fool young nobles tend to be. But a simple death does not warrant the presence of the King-Emperor."

"Quite…" The Archon's gaze fell once again on the gibbering creature. He shuddered in revulsion.

"If this monster is responsible, then put it to death. Such a thing does not deserve life, so foul is its countenance."

The crowd heard the king's words and jeered.

"They want blood, Archon. Why don't you give it to them?"

The creature raised itself upon shaky elbows and stared pitifully, raw pleading on features dominated by an awful beak—a nose so distorted and discoloured that Jhaz'Elrad's foot twitched involuntarily. *How I would like to plant it firmly between those close-set eyes and smash asunder.* "Well?"

The Archon's mammoth jowls quivered. "As ever, Eminence, things are not as simple as they appear. I believe this thing is known to you. It is called… *Scowl.*"

Jhaz'Elrad nodded. The name had recently come to his attention. He never normally listened to the dreary Spymaster—a small, dead-eyed Oldivian—or read his even duller reports, but the name had caught his interest. "If this is indeed Scowl, I now know why his reputation is so loathsome."

The monster's head twitched; it dribbled and choked. A ruin of a face lay half-hidden by a swathe of thick hair shining reddish-black in the flickering cresset-light. Hands clasped and unclasped as if searching for something.

The gathering hooted and wailed, anger rising to a crescendo. The King-Emperor lifted his black-fenneral sceptre, and the crowd, eager to get on, immediately quieted. Below, the ominous boom of waves sounded against the castle walls. Rain beat upon wooden shutters. In the distance, a hefty door banged in the whistling wind.

The Archon pulled himself up to his full height and gestured to a thin weasel of a man in the King-Emperor's own weavery. "Captain Shyk, his Eminence grows impatient. Your report please."

Shyk, swarthy, unshaven, with a weak chin and rat-like eyes proudly displayed a bandaged arm. "My liege." He bowed deeply before addressing the court, his voice a reedy sneer. "Part of my duties are to patrol the harbour town for vagabonds, drifts and—*unsuitables* who land unwanted upon our shores. After all, we cannot allow everyone free access to our fair land, now can we?" He smiled, revealing a set of yellow and black teeth.

The gathering showed its agreement vigorously.

"A loud disturbance brought my attention to the Lower End," Skyk continued, seemingly eager to retell his tale, "where, to my horror, I found this creature in violent disagreement with the young noble, Radd Krall. There was quite a crowd around the disturbance and, as is my duty, Eminence, I tried to make word and break the argument. When Radd pulled back the monster's hood, it looked at me with such an abhorrence of features that I knew my life was in danger. I lunged at it, but the thing had an unnatural weapon that smashed my sword. In the same motion, this dark blade stabbed Radd Krall through, pinning him to the quayside. Killed him dead as I watched. I'm not slow to act, Eminence, I hit the creature hard, knocking it over and, thankfully, he dropped that evil sword into the harbour. Without its weapon, a sort of change came over it. Knew he'd met his better, I suppose, although it took me and many brave helpers to disarm him of a smaller blade. Cut me up a treat." He proffered his injured arm again as evidence.

The Archon pursed fleshy lips, his eyes wet and intent. "Have you any notion what this disagreement was about?"

"None, other than it ended in poor Radd Krall's death. I would've finished the monster there and then, but I know your rules." Shyk looked at the prone wretch with undisguised malice. "This creature was a passenger upon a recently arrived ship. The same ship as the murdered noble."

"Thank you, Captain." Jhaz'Elrad leaned in close to the Archon. "This is all very interesting, *Archon Jarvid Glave,*" he whispered. "But I am losing my patience."

The Archon baulked for the first time. It was said that if Jhaz'Elrad used your full name, it would be written on your tombstone soon after. He swallowed hard. "King-Emperor," he replied with all the reverence he could muster. "It was not my will to summon you, but the law states that only the king can grant a reprieve and this matter is… complicated."

"You want me to set this vile monster free?"

Before the Archon could answer, an old man approached the throne, a gnarled wooden staff held high before him. Intent blue eyes sparkled from a ruddy, weathered face framed by voluminous silver hair and an impressive white beard. "If I may be permitted to speak," he said, his voice powerful and loud for one so aged.

The King-Emperor recognised him. *Dracus Krall. An ambitious noble who long ago fell foul of my father's court. What does the old fool want?*

Glave nodded. "Say your piece, Dracus, the King-Emperor is waiting."

The old man bowed, although his eyes remained fixed on Jhaz'Elrad. "The guilt of this creature is not in doubt, King-Emperor, but I have come to this Reeve to request weregild for my dead son, Radd Krall."

The chamber exploded in uproar.

"He was slain guiltless," continued Dracus, "and as such I claim a price be paid for this action. The Archon has many powers, but only you, my King, can grant me this boon. "

"A weregild, you say? How very, very interesting." The King-Emperor glared at Glave who shrugged. Be-ringed fingers stroked thoughtfully at his elegantly trimmed beard. "Do you not demand his death?"

"What I demand is not so unreasonable, if you will let me explain my motives, oh wise one."

The King-Emperor nodded and the crowd sank back into expectant silence.

"I know this creature you all abhor." Dracus' eyes played over the twitching, prisoner. "His name is Scowl, yet in far lands and courts he has many other names. He is *Blackbeak*, the *Iron-bane*, the *Hooded Scourge of Delving*. He is dark; marked by the Gyre and is not as we see him now for he is incomplete. He roams the land in search of woe, seeking out the unforgettable arts of delving to which he is inextricably bound. It is his purpose to find such vile works and destroy them."

A flash from the open windows and thunder rumbled from high above. The idiot upon the floor shivered and moaned.

"This is indeed most fascinating," said the King-Emperor with feigned disinterest, "please, do carry on."

Dracus bowed. "For many generations my family has held a murky secret, something so shadowy and worrisome that we have dared not speak of it openly." The old man's hypnotic voice reverberated in the Reeving Chamber, hissing around the smooth walls with a trailing whisper like that of a serpent. "A creature from the far past bedevils us, haunts our ancestral home of Keep Krall. A golem of watery flesh created by delving, a murderous thing bent upon the obliteration of our family."

The gathering drew back in horror. Cressets flickered, casting ghostly shadows in the gloom.

"It prevailed against all attempts at its destruction, and my House is prevented from returning to halls that were crafted for living and joy. The King-Emperor may not be aware, but I am an accomplished scribe. I find pleasure in history and myth, in augury and oracle. On an old, yellowed family parchment, a renowned seer foretold that the slayer of this golem would one day arrive unwanted in this land, and that woe would surround him. I heard of Scowl's presence upon the Oldivan Isles and dispatched Radd to find him. My son was as ever rash and unbelieving. How I regret the day I sent a mere boy on an old man's errand. How *unwanted* can this Scowl be to me?" He bowed his head in anguish.

"My weregild is this: release the prisoner, return his evil weapons and dispatch him at once to destroy this golem—as is his wont!"

The King-Emperor's face darkened.

"Despite appearances," the Archon whispered to Jhaz'Elrad, "and the boasts of those who captured him, this Scowl is a powerful warrior, dangerous and unworldly."

"Just look at it; I see no danger in this poor, twisted wretch."

The Archon's head gave the barest twitch to the negative. "I have also taken counsel from the Spymaster. We both agree. There is more to this Scowl than meets the eye. We should think twice before we release such a creature into the protection of someone who craves power so openly."

Jhaz'Elrad breathed deeply. "For once, Archon, I agree. But as you know full well, my hands are tied in this matter. Now finish this. I am a busy man."

Glave bowed and turned his attention back to the chamber. "That is indeed a revelation, Dracus Krall, I better understand the many enigmas of your family, and the shadow cast upon you and your kin. The King-Emperor is honour-bound to comply with your wishes but—this creature, this Scowl—can you be sure of its compliance?"

Dracus Krall's eyes narrowed. "I mourn my son, but I also mourn all my family dead. I would place them all against my belief in Scowl's destiny. The King-Emperor cannot deny me this request. Radd was of my blood and is my blood. The weregild must be given."

Jhaz'Elrad rose to his feet. "So be it."

"If my King-Emperor will grant me one more request?"

"I understand you are grieving, Dracus Krall," said Jhaz'Elrad with menace, "but do not take liberties with your King. It is enough that against my will and better judgment I grant you this weregild. Do not risk my further displeasure." He fingered his heavy sceptre, the symbol of his authority.

"I would never risk your discontent, Eminence," Dracus replied bowing. "I ask only that my brother-daughter, Vareena, accompany the quest, to see it done. I have trust in her. A long time ago, my greatest ancestor sealed Keep Krall with an enchantment. Its knowledge passed down from first born to first-born, from father to son and father to daughter. That knowledge now rests with her. Only she, as guardian of that knowledge, can open the Keep of Krall."

Jhaz'Elrad stared into the old man's eyes, yet could not divine his purpose. "Guardian or not, you would send a child on an adult's quest?" he asked with ill-disguised irritation.

A shout brought the King-Emperor's attention to a girl in her late teens standing close to Dracus Krall. She was tall, her noble birth showing in high cheekbones and defiant eyes shining emerald green even in the smoky gloom of the chamber. She wore the light-brown weave of a fighter: tightly fitting functional leathers that did nothing to diminish her well-proportioned limbs. A well-crafted yet discoloured sword of fenneral, the weapon-stone, rested at her side, its individual crystal facets catching flashes from the cresset-light. Lank-blonde hair hung upon her shoulders.

Jhaz'Elrad's eye was pleased at her beauty, hidden, as it was, behind a boyish demeanour.

Undaunted, Vareena spoke up, her voice loud and adamant. "I've no understanding why my uncle has chosen weregild, nor why he should choose to reveal family secrets to open Reeve. But I'm no child. If it's his wish for me to accompany the quest—then so be it."

Dracus placed a protective arm around Vareena's muscled shoulders, his eyes unwavering. "I must humbly ask for my king's apology. I do not wish to force his hand. But he must understand my family have been waiting generations for the fulfilment of this prophecy."

The Archon whispered once again in the King-Emperor's ear. "We cannot allow this creature freedom to roam our lands. Nor give in to Dracus' obvious ambition."

Jhaz'Elrad shrugged, catching the eye of his favourite courtier. "As you know full well, I do not share your interest in the affairs of state. I prefer the simpler pleasures." *Here is a perfect opportunity for my power-hungry Archon to earn his keep.* "Do what you will."

The Archon bowed. "Thank you Eminence. This will not end here, I promise."

Jhaz'Elrad addressed the chamber. "It is a dangerous game you play, Dracus Krall." He let his eyes roam over the tight form of Vareena and frowned. "Try to make sure you do not lose many more family members, or your House will fall..." He descended the steps and strutted out of the Reeving Chamber. Behind him, the gathering erupted into discussion.

BLACKBEAK

VAREENA KRALL made her way down into the deep warren of Castle Fangarra. A bleak place built high upon an elongated headland. Pointed spires jutted up from a buttress of shiny obsidian—like teeth from a wolf's blackened jawbone. Hence its fanciful name. Far below, the sea pounded and smashed against the ebony-coloured rock and slowly yielding walls.

This was Oldiva, the far most western land of Arn's northern continent. It scythed into a cold sea that provided most of their living, for this was a barren land where bare slate held the sway over rare clumps of evergreen. Trade with the Unbidden Isles and the southern dominions of Domarland, Gula and K'Bith made for a more market-based economy, but if not for Ariva to the east, there would be nothing other than dried fish to survive the bad seasons.

Like all lands upon Arn, Oldiva changed under the Gyre. Now, as the extended summer of Goldering ended, it had become a forsaken place of freezing rains and harsh sea gales.

The under-keep was a pokey maze of hidden alcoves

and snakelike tunnels. In the coming winter months of Bluster, these passages would fill with those eager to survive the near constant blizzards that buried everything under hundreds of feet of snow. Families lived where they could until the snowfall became thick enough to carve out snow-homes. Every day, new mouths arrived keen for repayment of the levy—a hoard of dried fish, wheat, meats and berries stored in immense larders. Food enough to feed the castle and its levyers through the bad seasons. Until those snows arrived, accommodation was in short supply. Disputes were commonplace and the under-castle a place to be avoided.

Decked and ready for the journey, her favourite sword of fenneral at her side, Vareena appeared especially menacing. And that's what confused her. Uncle Dracus frowned upon her tomboyish ways. Being a woman of noble birth, it was a constant battle for her to resist the many arrangements of the court.

He's up to something, thought Vareena, furrowing her brows. *Why else would Dracus reveal the family shame before the King-Emperor and set me on what he considers such an 'unwomanly' task?* Vareena knew the answer: *Only I hold the hidden enchantment of opening. Only I may enter that imposing ruin of rock and stone. Not that I want to.* Dracus had tried to extract the secret from her, but she'd resisted. *I promised my father to never reveal that knowledge, and I'll not break such a sacred vow.*

Keep Krall once outshone Castle Fangarra. For countless generations this golem had eroded her family's power and influence that, if not so tainted, could have rivalled Jhaz'Elrad himself. Dracus often reminded her of this. Her family had waited many passes of the Gyre for this Scowl. No matter how she may resent the responsibility, she did not have the power to refuse. *If I am anything, I am a Krall. I may dislike my uncle, but I will not let my father's House down.*

With heavy feet and low spirits, she reached the dungeon level—a rank place regularly flooded by the sea. The weasel-like captain waited for her.

"Greetings Vareena Krall," Shyk said, flicking his small, black eyes over her leather-clad body, his nasal voice amplified in the confined space. "And my commiserations on your sad loss."

Vareena furrowed her eyebrows, unwilling to discuss her unfortunate cousin. She knew the militia well, and how their gossip often featured the brother-daughter of Dracus Krall. Some of it angry that a noble woman was allowed to wander the castle dressed provocatively in fighting weaves, others salacious and unsavoury. Shyk's performance at the Reeve had done nothing to commend him. She found his small-mindedness difficult to tolerate. *And if he looks at me like that one more time, he'll feel the flat of my blade where he least wants it.*

"It's a sad business, this. I'd welcome the chance to finish the fiend, yet—"

Vareena drew breath and shook her head. *I hate to admit it, but I agree with the nasty little captain.* "Where is the creature?"

"Come."

She didn't relish the impending meeting, yet her uncle had assured Vareena that this Scowl wasn't the idiot he seemed—and Dracus never made idle statements. She followed Shyk into a cell lit by a single cresset. Tense-looking militiamen jumped to attention.

The creature sat in a corner, a twisted rope the width of her thigh snaking around his ankle from a worn hole in the cell's rock wall. The thing lifted a shaky head and stared right at her. Vareena stepped backwards. Scowl's face was even more hideous close up—its features distorted—as if they'd been smashed and hastily put back together. The nose was a black, discoloured beak, on either side of which two iron-blue yet intelligent eyes squatted unevenly.

Shyk rubbed his injured arm. "I have my orders, Vareena Krall, but are you absolutely sure?"

"I'm not sure at all, Captain. This is my uncle's weregild. If it were up to me, I'd order you to dispatch this thing here and now."

The men murmured approvingly.

Vareena sighed, letting her hand rest on the pommel of her sword. "Alas, that cannot be. We must return his weapons." Her voice reverberated off the walls—noble, precise and containing a natural tone of command. *I sound like my uncle.*

"In truth, Vareena," whispered the captain, "its sword is a dark thing. The poniard the same. Evil. I fear to return them. The man who retrieved them from the harbour has become a madman. It does not bode well."

"You have ten men here, more outside. I see no palpable danger from this thing."

"I've seen him fight," he whispered.

"It must be done," said Vareena, hating her own words. "'Tis the will of my uncle and the King-Emperor."

The captain sighed. "So be it—Bring out the box!" he barked.

Vareena unfastened the peace-knot upon her sword. A stone, sarcophagus-like chest was dragged into the cell and set to rest on the floor next to the prisoner. Shyk cursed under his breath and pulled back the lid. A shadow seemed to inhabit the box, a blackness covering a strange selection of objects. The soldiers ungirded their fenneral swords in alarm.

The creature's breathing changed, slowed. Scowl reached inside and grasped the most evil object Vareena had ever seen. A thickly hewn sword, long in the hilt and sabre-like. A filigree of shapes and glyphs traced the dark surface for almost two thirds of its length. Here snags jutted—designed to catch unwary blades. The remainder was shiny grey and scythed, polished to a blinding excellence.

Something living seemed to dwell in the weapon. Moving? She could not be sure. *Almost liquid. It is as I suspected. His weapon is crafted from irons, from delving metals. She shivered. Such things are wicked, forbidden.*

With its taking, the creature changed in demeanour. The face was still an ugly mask but the limbs uncurled to become strong and lithe, the muscles no longer fighting one another—as if they were drawing strength from the grey metal's touch.

Vareena blinked. The creature—the man—was young. *My age.*

Scowl stood on powerful legs. Gone was the gibbering wretch and in its place, a tall, disfigured youth. Authority, surprising grace and a fierce pride shone from within, along with the unmistakable taint of danger. Vareena noticed Scowl's left forearm and hand were withered, the fingers stubby and childlike. He held the blade with his good hand and spun it around him like a living thing. A delicate limning of gold caught the cresset-light—the weapon revealed itself as a thing of beauty and grand design. The sword of a hero. The blade twisted again and became foreboding, shadowy and evil. It stridulated weirdly, keening and buzzing with a cadence that spoke of delving and the unnatural arts. The sword danced, slicing through the rope binding his ankle and returned inert to his thigh.

"By the Smokes!" Shyk gasped. His men jumped back in alarm.

"Do not be afraid." Scowl's nasal voice was unexpectedly powerful, but contained a complete lack of joy. The air struggled with its passing. He turned and faced Vareena. "I know of our quest. I am ready."

"All is prepared," replied Vareena, her voice trembling, despite her best efforts.

Scowl reached again into the chest and removed an iron poniard of the same outlandish design as his scythe. Iron-blue eyes pained at the touch but relief soon followed. He dressed quickly, sable weavery fitting him with the intimacy of long use. Black breaches, undershirt and tunic. He draped a cape around his shoulders and, pushing his thick raven-coloured hair away from his face, pulled a hood over his head, his nose protruding behind the fabric like some awful beak. His twisted mouth remained uncovered, sitting atop a strong chin, his only good feature. He took out a bundle and a few other possessions and girded them. "We leave now."

"What are you?" Vareena Krall whispered, the words coming unbidden to her lips.

The answer, when it came, was full of pain. *"What indeed?"*

BANDITS

"SO GIRL, you would rather me dead?" The words were lifeless, spoken without emotion.

Behind Scowl, the Sun sank below the horizon. A bloated blaze of red and orange, half-hidden by an array of thin clouds drifting in the distance. The Sun's sister, Eltirren, was just as big and bright in the sky, but her light possessed no warming. She was Coldstar, *Bringer of Light;* her presence extended the gloaming for many hours. With the passing months, her reign would increase, with night becoming nothing more than a fleeting moment between rising and setting suns and the time of the Whitenight would begin.

Vareena shuddered. Castle Fangarra was many leagues behind them. They had left the King's militia at the city's gates. *Had he waited for the harsher light of Coldstar to frame his words?*

A sound that might have been a twisted laugh died upon the air. "It was difficult to miss your hatred as you talked within the dungeon," he continued.

"I don't know who or what you are," said Vareena, her normal, confident tones muted. "And I don't want to."

He is not the first man who thinks he can intimidate me. I'm a noble from a once-great family. He should do well to remember that. "If you're about to do me harm then let's stop here and have it out!" She turned to face him, planting her feet apart, her hand resting on the hilt of her sword. Anger tinged with fear shone from her emerald eyes.

Blackbeak twitched his misshapen head towards her.

Long moments passed. The wind blew insidiously. Somewhere in the distance, a lone wolf howled into the extended afternoon.

Iron-blue eyes shone from two jagged holes cut into the rough fabric of Scowl's improvised hood. They betrayed no feeling. "You think I am more than just a man?"

Vareena was unprepared for the question. "I've not seen anything—*anyone* like you before. You killed my cousin. You carry weapons that mark you as strange and dangerous. Of course I think you different."

"I am sorry about your cousin's death. He was a fool. But yes..." He walked away. *"I am marked."* Vareena hurried after him. "Is it wrong for me to hate you? Is it?"

"Hate is an easy emotion. It does not sit well in you."

"I have a cheery temperament. That much is true"

"Then perhaps you can suspend your dislike until this quest be done."

Vareena tightened her gird-belt and adjusted the heavy pack upon her shoulders. Wind tugged at her lank, blonde hair. "I don't hate you, but I have no love for your company. I cannot go against my family, against the House of Krall. And you did kill my cousin."

Scowl said nothing.

"Do not misunderstand me, but in truth, I did not care for Radd," she said, wondering why she was confiding in her cousin's murderer. But Radd had told her the answer many times: 'You're an arrogant little blabbermouth, Vareena. You may think you know everything, but you don't. Why father hasn't married you off to some fat, rich merchant, I do not know.' "My cousin was a bore, a bully and a loud-mouth," she said. "If it hadn't been you who killed him, someone else would have."

Blackbeak stepped forward at a faster gait. "Tell me more of your… guardianship and this golem."

"I have little interest in this quest, or in Keep Krall," she spat into the cold air.

"It would seem you are short upon any sentiment, but please, continue."

Vareena sighed, her shoulders dropping as the anger left her. "I'd hoped to leave its memory behind. My father died there. He wanted to talk with this golem-beast… the Gyre knows why." She tried to be flippant, but heartache tinged her words.

"Ah yes, the creature of delving." Scowl breathed in deeply, as if relishing the meeting to come.

"In return the golem took his arm, wrenched it from him as a child might maim its dolly. He was able to escape and close the keep once again, but he died from his injuries." Her voice sounded disdainful. "Uncle Dracus knew nothing of the guardianship or of the secret enchantment used to open its closed doors and was furious with my father for keeping it secret from him. But of more pain to him was the loss of the Ring of Souls—" Vareena stopped in mid-sentence, alarm showing in her face.

"The Ring of Souls?"

"Nothing more than a family heirloom. A ring passed down from first-born to first-born," she said. *No one in my family knows I possess it, a gift from my father just before he died. He made me promise to keep the ring a secret.* "With it went the secret of opening, the enchantment," she added with quick words. "My Father was wearing the ring when the golem wrenched his arm from his body. It was lost forever. My uncle pleaded with my father to tell him the enchantment before he gasped his last breath. Yet he revealed the incantation to me only and forbade me upon his deathbed to tell any other but my own first-born. How I rue that day. A day that has led me here, to this road… to you."

Scowl grunted disapproval. At what, Vareena could not tell. "Your uncle is indeed an ambitious man."

"Maybe, but he and father did not get on. He went to Keep Krall on his own. Dracus was livid."

Scowl's head twitched to one side. "You have barely spoken since we left the city, now it seems you can't wait to blurt out family secrets."

Vareena's cheeks flushed with embarrassment. "I've always been like this. Since a child. Father called me his 'little chatterbox'."

"Then tell me more."

"In truth, it's a relief to get these words off my chest. When father died, I too became moribund. So important was my secret that even when Dracus told me I was also dying, I still could not share it. I wouldn't willingly send anyone else to suffer my father's gruesome fate. Luckily, I recovered." Vareena sighed into the icy air.

"Luck indeed."

"But what of you, Scowl? What's your tale?"

"A long story."

"I am always eager to learn. My tutors all told me I'm the cleverest student they had ever had," she said, sounding more like a precocious child than a refined noble-girl. "But I'm curious—and you are a mystery. Your accent is like none I have ever heard. Where are you from?"

"From no land on Arn."

"Don't speak in riddles. I know all the lands on both continents. I've memorised them all."

"You will not find my home on any map, girl. It is a place full of arcane wonders, a land beyond your simple imaginings. A world where delving has gone mad."

"I don't understand."

"And you never shall."

Vareena shrugged. "And—your weapon?"

"IronScythe is her name."

A sleek hawk screeched above, attacking an enormous crow. Feathers fell around them like blackened snow. Vareena shivered at the sight. "What is she? This IronScythe?"

"A weapon crafted for vengeance from iron that manacled hate and retribution. She is power. She is revenge."

"But metals are forbidden. Everyone knows that."

"Can you be so sure?"

"I don't know." Her voice was young and presumptuous. "But I saw you in the cell. You are nothing without metal's touch."

He stared across the snow-covered plain to the small hills looming ahead. "We are all *nothing*, girl. All of us. Nothing."

Night passed under an inky, blustery shroud that Vareena found intolerable. Scowl slept outside, his rasping loud even through the thick walls of her hidebound tent. Thankfully, the time between dusk and dawn was shorter in this season. As the first warmer light of the

Sun breached the sky, she emerged tired, but ready to continue.

The new day brought no joy. At Sun-midday, six hours before the rising of Eltirren, Scowl spotted a group of men about twenty minutes' walk away. "Is travelling safe here?"

"We are on the Eastern Road. A merchant route. There hasn't been an attack since I can remember. We should be safe enough and, besides, I'm a trained swordswoman." She clapped her hand on the hilt of her stone blade with pride.

"Then we will continue."

Scowl's faith in her judgement impressed her, yet as the band of men approached, Vareena moved closer to him. *Something feels wrong.* She undid the peace-knot upon her sword and kept her hand ready.

"Say nothing," Scowl rasped. "This situation does not require your precocious, noble tones."

Vareena frowned. "Is there something wrong with the way I speak?"

"You are loud, over-bearing, over-confident and verbose. Dracus schooled you well. Keep your mouth closed."

"Oh."

"Be silent!"

Shocked by his sudden anger, she clamped her mouth shut and stared ahead. Vareena counted nine men… and nine was an uncomfortable number. Swarthy, unwashed, their weaves were stained and dirty, their swords gleamed with cleaning oils.

The road was nothing more than a worn pathway— less covered by stones than the surrounding plain.

Scowl gave them a respectful berth, but the men

came towards him.

"Now, who do we have here then?" asked their leader, staring at Scowl's hooded features.

The men had smeared mud across their faces and weaves. Many of them had facial scars.

A sign of long practice with the sword and common for those in the militia, thought Vareena. *They are not what they seem.*

Blackbeak remained silent. He carried on walking as if the men were invisible.

A thick-ridged scar twisted the leader's mouth into a half-smile. "You ignore me?" he said. "Now that's just plain bad manners."

"What is he hiding?" one of the men jeered.

"Perhaps his beauty is too noble, too refined for us common folk!" cried another.

Laughter followed the remark.

"Be gone," commanded Vareena, disturbed and disappointed at Scowl's silence. "We travel upon an errand for the King-Emperor—you would do well to respect that."

"An errand of the King you say?" The leader's tone changed. The laughing ceased.

Scowl stopped dead in his tracks and turned.

"So a friend of that fool Jhaz'Elrad tries to hide from us? You'll bring us a large ransom." He nodded to his men who drew their swords.

"No, you misunderstand, we—" Vareena was hit a vicious blow that sent her sprawling.

"And some tight upper-class arse for the lads. Nice."

The men laughed again, turning towards Scowl who remained mute, unmoving.

"Hello in there!" taunted the scarred leader. "Come

out, come out, whoever you are!"
His laugh turned into a cry of surprise.
Iron flashed in the sunlight.

Ring of Souls

BLOOD DRENCHED the road in crimson. The leader's arm lay on the ground, its loss unbalancing him. Scowl was not finished. Vareena looked on dumbfounded. The blade spun and took the man's head clean off.

IronScythe sang, held firm and sure in Scowl's good hand. The other bandits jumped back in alarm, trying to evade the deadly blade. One misjudged his distance. Scowl flicked his sword in and out—a murderous lunge that pierced ribcage, heart and backbone. The attacker was dead before he realised his mistake. In the same movement, the hooded demon rolled forward. He landed in a crouch, bringing IronScythe jutting up through another's groin and stomach. He twisted her viciously. Blood and the contents of a last meal spilled. A lunge backwards, and yet another fell to the touch of the dark metal.

Two more bandits came at him. Blackbeak parried, IronScythe slicing the tip off one crystalline weapon and slamming sideways into the other. The incredulous man's sword shattered into a thousand flashing gems. Blackbeak butted him in the face with the iron-hilt. The second attacker rushed forward with his now blunted blade and over-committed himself. A hacked midriff was his punishment—iron sliced through his spine. Scowl kicked him to the ground, whirling around to finish off his blood-splattered companion.

Seven of the bandits lay dead or dying.

A muffled scream and Scowl turned to find one of the two remaining men holding Vareena in a vice-like grip. The other held a stiletto-like crystal blade to her throat. Before Scowl could act, the bandit leapt backwards, throwing his glass dagger aside as if it was alive.

For the barest of seconds, a dark band appeared upon the exposed finger of Vareena's right hand before disappearing again.

Blackbeak pulled out his poniard and flung—the iron thudded sickly into gristle and neck bones. The man dropped, gurgling.

The last bandit released Vareena and stood back in defeat, arms raised.

IronScythe had not finished. She whipped through the air, taking the man's sword arm at the elbow. He squealed, falling into the dirt.

Scowl wiped the scythe free of blood and sheathed the weapon in his scabbard.

The surviving bandit, clutching his bloody stump, upped and ran. Iron-blue eyes followed him, Scowl's head occasionally twitching.

Vareena retched. "Is that how you killed Radd?" she croaked.

"Do not remind me of that fool," Blackbeak said, crouching next to her. "And you're right… you cannot seem to keep your noble mouth shut. The next time, remember to do what I say. You might not be so lucky. Here." Scowl proffered the leader's weapon; a wonderful thing, well-crafted and made of the purest white fenneral. "This sword has too much worth to be left behind. The grain is faultless. See how strength comes from crystals in perfect alignment? Iron cannot shatter such stone. Take it."

"No."

He thrust the sword, hilt first. "Don't be a fool."

"Alright!" Vareena snatched the fine fenneral from his outstretched hand. Larger than her sword, yet perfectly balanced, its weight fuelled her fighting arm. The finest blade she had ever held. "I don't understand," she said, marvelling at the perfect crystalline array. "This is a champion's prize, not the weapon of a bandit. That's why I had no chance against such men. It's rare for me to taken by surprise."

A sound that might have been a laugh escaped from Scowl's lips. "Trained you may be, but a fighter you are not. They were excellent swordsmen, mercenaries. They did not reckon on a contest with iron. King-Emperor Jhaz'Elrad was behind this attack, or at least one of his lackeys."

"What?"

"He suspects the motives of your Uncle, Vareena—as you should."

Vareena wiped tears from reddened eyes. *What have I got myself into the middle of?* The bitter stench of blood was over-powering, yet she could not help but respect Scowl's practiced butchery. *IronScythe is a supernatural thing. Worrisome. A weapon of devastating power.*

Blackbeak stalked away. His cape had remained free of gore, only his thick black boots were stained crimson.

They ascended a treacherous cliff-top road as night began to fall. The sea thundered somewhere below. Scowl had said nothing since the attack, standing impassive upon the cliff's edge, the steady crash of waves hollow and echoing as Vareena pitched her small tent.

"You saw it didn't you?" she asked.

"Of course I did. You may be noble trained and schooled, but you are not practised in lying. Your father did not lose the Ring of Souls. He gave it to you. And what a gift. It must be a simulacrum, a delusion-giver. A prize worthy of a queen. No wonder your uncle was so upset. You used the ring to cast an illusion on the bandit's blade—why else did he throw his dagger aside? An illusion hides it upon your finger even now."

"How can you know this?"

"I know many things—*Vareena*. Do not lie to me again."

The syllables of her name sounded perverse when uttered upon his lips. It turned her insides cold.

Blackbeak faced the sea.

Vareena watched him warily. "Am I—am I in danger from you?"

"You have far greater enemies."

"What does that mean?"

"If you have not worked that out for yourself, then you're not as intelligent as you think."

"The ring is mine, tell none about it."

"Goodnight Vareena. Make your tent. Sleep. For tomorrow we enter Keep Krall."

BRIDGE OF STONE

ROCK AND buildings jutted from a stark, angry ocean. Proud, stern and intractable, challenging the sky. A craggy, unreachable island crafted by both man and the constant deafening waves. Keep Krall squatted atop a needle of rock: an immense tree-like trunk of sea-ablated stone from which a canopy of fine towers, spires and improbable overhangs sprang forth with little regard for safety or gravity. Seagulls screeched, racing between tall pylons, riding the natural updrafts with nothing more than the tilt of an outstretched wing. Once gilded minarets and steeples, now bleached white by wind and sun, shone bright in the daylight.

"Your Keep seems wholesome, clean. Even magnificent," Blackbeak began. "Yet something evil and unforgiving crawls like a bloated maggot under its whited exterior."

Scowl and Vareena stood on a precipice twenty feet away from an impressive arched entranceway perched high and inaccessible. Once-magnificent double doors made of the hardest black wood sagged on their hinges, hanging above the drop. A hundred feet below, the sea surged relentlessly, pebbles and shells chattering between every crash. The Keep was isolated from both boat and land.

Silent, Vareena crossed her arms over her stomach. Keep Krall sickened her more than any bloody spectacle or carnage. The top-heavy mini-city had haunted her thoughts, her dreams and her conversations with her obsessive uncle since she was a child. *How many times had Dracus commanded me to come here with him?* She'd refused every entreaty. It had taken the king's Reeve and the death of her cousin to push her here.

Her companion viewed the magnificent Keep with the same disinterest he had shown when dispatching bandits the day before.

Behind the two travellers, a road cut a straight course through a tall promontory forming an artificial ravine. They were on a lip, a wide fanning overhang.

Scowl's hooded head twitched in her direction. "I am waiting, Vareena."

"First, I want to ask you something," she said. "I saw how easily you dealt with those attackers yesterday. So how come the Captain of the Guard, who is no swordsman, was able to defeat you?"

Blackbeak laughed, a peculiar reedy sound. "I am drawn by destiny. IronScythe is also drawn by that same force… it guides her blade as it guides me. I but follow. I am never surprised by circumstance, although I do not relish her loss. Now, if you are satisfied…" He nodded towards the chasm.

"The enchantment is something I cannot let you hear. This is my family's keep, not yours. You must go," she said as if dismissing one of her vassals.

Scowl bowed in exaggerated deference and retreated until she was satisfied by the distance.

Vareena felt absurd speaking the words she'd hidden for so long. Yet at the sound of the enchantment, a peculiar sense of belonging swept through her. *How many of my ancestors knew this verse, how many had used these same words, standing where I am standing now, with the wind in their hair, the sea crashing below?* She reached the end of her incantation and waited.

Nothing happened.

She repeated the chant. Still nothing. She glanced back at Scowl who nodded for her to continue.

She felt a fool, for try as she might, the words she had guarded almost all her life had no effect. She tried shouting the verses with abandon, but the gap remained.

Blackbeak came over to stand behind her.

"The enchantment does not work," she blurted.

The wind pushed the rough, black material of Scowl's hood against his sharp nose as he dropped a large boulder at his feet. Before she could ask what he was doing, he brushed her aside, unsheathing IronScythe and swung the arcane sword around his head with menace.

She gazed open-mouthed at the spectacle. The flashing blade that caught the fierce white light of the Coldstar and reflected it twice as bright.

"By the power of iron," Blackbeak yelled, his voice echoing around them, "I command thee, bridge—arise!"

She took a step back, and another. Scowl seemed preternatural, enlarged—displaying awesome power. Her throat became dry, her skin whitened.

A loud rumble filled the gully. An immense platform, befouled with seaweeds and clinging shellfish, appeared from beneath the water's surface, rising to form a bridge to Keep Krall's doors. Blackbeak faced her. Doom-ridden and dangerous.

"…How?" Vareena asked, dumbfounded.

Scowl pointed IronScythe at his feet.

She stared down, surprised to see an almost invisible ring in the smooth rock of the road. The dropped boulder sat within it. "I don't understand."

"The bridge is not controlled by any enchantment you possess." He sheathed IronScythe and stood back.

"What?"

"Only a Savant-master can place or use such majiks and you are not practiced in Usery."

"But—"

"This is a clear gully and an empty road. Suspicious then that three large boulders should sit here, all about the same size and weight. It did not take long to work out the mechanism of the drawbridge."

Vareena shook her head in disbelief. "But I am a Krall, not you. How can you find the way into my father's keep when my enchantment failed? I've guarded those words all my life."

"This keep was built during the Golden Age, Vareena, before delving brought ruin to the land. The stonework is neither low nor squat like many of its successors; it is crafted with high majesty. Not unlikely then, that the arts of machines and delving were employed in its design—and these heinous arts are known to me. While you uttered your useless verses, I placed boulders on two other pressure points."

"My father must have known this secret also. So why teach me the enchantment?"

"You are a quick learner and I guess he had little time. An enchantment would keep you safe. As I suspected—he lied to you."

"My father was no liar!" Vareena lurched forward,

thumping his chest with hard fists, but Scowl did not react. A step back and she caught him a blow to his sharp nose with a powerful right hook.

A scream of pain and Scowl pushed her to the floor. She fell heavily upon her back.

"He lied to protect you," Scowl whispered, blood leaking over his lips.

"What?"

"From the golem… and from your uncle."

"No! He taught me the enchantment upon his deathbed, made me promise never to reveal it. He wouldn't have lied! Not to me. You know nothing about him!"

"I have learnt much and can guess the rest."

Vareena scrambled backwards and found her feet. "Explain yourself!"

"Your father fathomed what Dracus was capable of if he found out Keep Krall could be opened. He guessed you were in mortal danger. Your father not only feared his brother, Vareena—but also the golem. He would not willingly tell you the real secret of the Keep's opening. Not after he witnessed the horror lurking in your ancestral home. Your father made you learn the enchantment and, in deceiving you, saved your life."

She shook her head, wanting to blot out the cold voice that filled her with so much pain.

"Do you really think that you'd still be alive if you had told your uncle the secret, or had not kept your precious ring hidden? And what of your cousin, Radd? Why should he try and enlist my interest by talking of a 'treasure hoard' beyond those keep doors?"

"Treasure?"

"Treasure enough to buy armies of men to topple King-Emperor Jhaz'Elrad. Dracus thinks he's playing a clever game, but his son gave too much away. And he did not reckon on the intervention of iron."

"So that's your interest? You seek this treasure for yourself?"

"I seek but one thing." He wiped at the steady stream of blood leaking from his hood. "To destroy all works of delving. This is my destiny, my reason for being. Without this quest... I am nothing."

The statement, although cold and unfeeling, was tinged with hurt.

"What do you mean?"

"I am not of this world, Vareena. In my true home, I am weak, moribund. A sad creature unable to leave his hospital bed. You saw me as I truly am back in the Reeving Chamber. A miserable wretch incapable of standing on his own two feet, powerless to even feed himself. But here, on this strange planet, I have IronScythe. She is my strength." Far below a large wave smashed into the cliff face, its sound echoing under the vaulted arch of the dripping, shell-encrusted bridge. Scowl's pained whisper continued, its timbre gaining in volume until it became one with the crashing sea. "I am pushed by the whim of the Gyre to find darkness and delving, to destroy evil and depravity, and to wear that particular ordure like a badge. I am marked by delving, as surely as I am made to destroy it. But listen well, Vareena, while you are under my care, no harm shall come to you. That much I promise."

Gusts of wind whipped at Vareena's lank hair. "I didn't mean to injure you."

"It is nothing."

"Let me see to it." She reached for his nose.

"No." He shook his head and moaned in pain.

In a few quick movements, Vareena untied and

removed his hood, forcing herself to stare impassively at the twisted features. She delicately dabbed at the blackened ruin of his nose with wadding taken from her pack. "You are not much to look upon," she joked.

A smile flashed across the bent, disfigured features, making brief sense of the deformity.

"You shouldn't be ashamed of your face," said Vareena. "You should show it proudly."

"A bold statement from one so unhindered by ugliness." He ran his half-hand down her cheek and, try as she might, Vareena couldn't prevent herself from cringing. He replaced his Scowl. "I wear this hood not for others, Vareena, but for myself. Now stay here." His good hand found the long hilt of IronScythe. "I will soon return."

Vareena's eyes flashed with confusion, flickering past his hood to stare at the rotting double doors of Keep Krall and back again to her enigmatic companion. "We're not going together?"

"The golem is an evil I will defeat alone."

"You think me incapable? I am noble-born and noble-trained."

"You are no doubt skilful with a blade. But already you have been tested on this journey and been found wanting. The rattle and crash of the practice arena cannot prepare you for real battle."

"I can handle myself. If you had not been so eager to use your blade, I could've dealt with those bandits—without my sword."

"I doubt that very much."

"Then see this!"

The air shimmered around the young girl, colours twisting and turning. Changing. The clatter of surging waves became distorted, echoing peculiarly until...

Vareena was no more. In place of the teenager, stood a tall, muscular warrior bedecked in blackened armour, dented and stained with the blood of fresh battle. He held a gore-covered battle-axe at shoulder height—ready to slice asunder. Red eyes stared out of a scarred, grizzled face framed by a magnificent horned helm, a growl upon lips that quivered and foamed with the berserker.

Scowl stood his ground, impassive to the enormous brute now standing before him. The air shimmered again and the warrior disappeared.

"You're... not impressed?" Vareena said, crestfallen.

"Do you think you can defeat a golem with such party-tricks? You hardly touch the power of your illusion ring."

A mix of rage and humiliation lurched across Vareena's face. Her eyebrows made a furious marriage, her green eyes sparkling with fury. "This is my family's weregild, Scowl. You'd be dead if not for my uncle. You do my bidding. Understand? It is my destiny to enter this Keep and I shall do so."

"Come then," he said. "If you are so eager to meet your ancestor, I will not delay you." He grabbed her arm and marched her over the slippery bridge to the impressive but age-ridden keep doors, the hinges split, torn asunder by their own decaying weight.

"Get off me!"

"Look," he said, pointing his ruined hand at an elegantly wrought motto carved into the lintel above the archway, a circle of white stone in which an ingot of black-fenneral had formed naturally in the shape of a swooping krall—a magnificent black-eagle common to these lands. He lifted up Vareena's hand. The Ring of Souls was of the same design. "This gives you the right to enter Keep Krall. Not your uncle's weregild. This is your inheritance, Vareena. If you are fool enough to enter, despite my advice, I cannot stop you."

She pulled free. "What do you mean?"

Scowl unsheathed IronScythe. "Please, your permission to break these doors down."

"My permission?"

"Your ring marks you as Keep Mistress."

"Krall is mine?"

Scowl nodded. "Do you now understand? Your heirloom would give you dominion of its halls at any Reeve. Not your uncle, Dracus."

"But that's impossible, he'd never allow it."

"Dracus is not Krall's Master and never was. You are the direct heir, Vareena."

"Then…"

"Yes. Once I destroy this golem, only you will stand in the way of his ambition."

"But I don't want it. This place was always a dream, a nightmare to me. My father died here. I want nothing to do with it."

"What you want will make no difference to him."

Vareena stared at the combined beauty of natural rock and excellent stonemasonry rearing high above her. "So it is Dracus I must fear. That's why he didn't marry me off. And if not for the enchantment, I'd be dead. You were right, Scowl. Father saved my life. I'm sorry I hit you."

Blackbeak waved IronScythe with impatience. "Do I have your permission, Mistress?"

This Scowl is a strange mixture of dark power, riddles and vulnerability—Am I beginning to trust him? "Yes, go ahead."

The She-blade battered into the wood, booming

into the empty halls behind.

Vareena took a step back. "The golem will come."

"I would guess the fiend knows of our presence. Already it fears the touch of vengeful iron."

Another resounding boom and the doors exploded inwards—a pile of rotting planks and mould-covered leather. In an instant, Scowl was inside. "Come." Blackbeak stepped forwards, unworried by the gloom. Moving stealthily in the near black.

Vareena followed, drawing her new sword. "You do not fear the dark?" She peered after him, fearing hidden pits or the golem's sinewy fingers at her throat.

"Yes, darkness is delving's friend." Scowl stopped. "But not for long." He lifted his iron blade and pointed to one of the empty cressets lining the walls. And in a voice that seemed to come from the air itself, he chanted:

> *strand o' warmth*
> *strand o' light*
> *bon long and bon true*
> *eso arc es tranbrand grat*
> *eso attik es a' echu!*

The cresset flamed into sudden life, sparking and burning with quick, bright light, bathing the entrance hall in crazy shadows.

Vareena was astonished. Scowl's words seemed to pass somewhere beyond this dimension. A cant of the Branding Crafting, but in no tongue she'd heard before. Every Keep and Snowhall possessed Brandsmen, whose duty was to light braziers and fires. Only the adept could accomplish what she had just seen.

"Now, let us find this golem beast, for IronScythe

burns in my hand!" Blackbeak removed a stranding from his pack, lighting the dried brand from the cresset and handed her the flickering flame.

A change was coming over Scowl. A murkier aspect revealed under the cant of evocation and dancing, orange flame.

Already Vareena fancied she could see the golem's doom in the iron-blue eyes that squinted through his torn hood. In them rested the power of retribution, a doom-ridden authority that could not be smitten by darkness and delving alone.

Was destiny calling him?

Somewhere within the Keep of her ancestors, the golem shivered.

GOLEM

THEY ENTERED fantastic corridors, overlaid with marbled-arranx, a deep brown luscious stone shining like polished rosewood. The tiles caught sparkles of light from Vareena's torch and released them in star-pointed rainbow bursts. The ceiling crawled with carvings that danced with their passing. Doors revealed themselves as mammoth creations of black-grey stone mimicking fenneral. Floors, paved in crimson and azure and white, were soft and yielding underfoot. Vareena was enchanted, mesmerised. For a time she forgot the creature, the golem of Krall lurking somewhere below.

They passed into a large chamber, gliding in the gloom like ghosts of floating light. Cobwebs swayed. Spiders scuttled amongst furniture half-crumbled into dust. Once magnificent tapestries, now full of holes, their colours faded by rot, hung drunkenly on ancient walls.

Many such openings and passages did they enter. Many rooms and alcoves. A swirling mass of beauty and confusion. "How do you know where to go?" she asked when she found her voice.

Scowl breathed in deeply. "Think of me like a bloodhound. The golem lurks somewhere below. I smell its foul ordure. Come, I am eager to get this deed done."

Vareena was once again reminded of the horror that had pulled her father asunder and murdered him. *This is no place of the living—It's a crypt.*

They arrived at a massive pair of doors above which perched an impressive glass arch inlaid with precious stones. Vareena gasped at the sheer wealth those gems alone represented. They passed underneath, arriving in the Great Hall. Every keep and castle on the world of Arn had a similar chamber, used for banqueting, festivals and ceremony, but never had Vareena seen such a magnificent room. Colossal, rounded and twice the size of anything Castle Fangarra could offer. Marbled walls curved up to a vaulted arch. Light poured through countless openings. A wondrous banqueting hall where generations ago all had eaten and been merry.

Their footfalls echoed in the dimness, their breath bounced off far walls and high ceilings—the cauldron of this place magnified even the rustling of their weaves. Impassive as ever, Scowl headed for the Kitchens.

A chill filled Vareena's soul.

The Kitchens were connected to enormous underground vaults known collectively as *The Larders.* Here, the levy was stored against the bad times. Bluster and Tranquillity were the two longest seasons of the gyre forcing keep-folk to spend many months trapped beneath snows four times the height of their Keep. A regular supply of vittles was paramount to survival. In the opposite season of Blaze, when the land roasted and burned, these vaults provided a cool haven for succulent fruits and grains.

Vareena shivered, lagging behind. In all keeps and castles in every land, the Larders doubled as a vast playground for the keep's many children. In them, the monsters of her childhood imagination dwelled. *But here, the monster is real.*

Blackbeak grabbed her with his half-hand, dragging her forward. "You will be safer with me, Vareena. A monster it may be, but I have mastered more powerful foes. This is what I am crafted for."

His words stabbed with cold asperity. Down they went, down into the murk, down into the bowels of Keep Krall, down into the lair of the golem.

A cerulean-tinged glow from bluish moulds growing on walls and ceiling rendered the torch useless. The unnatural light had a taint of sepulchre.

Vareena glanced at Scowl and killed the flame, dropping the smoking brand to the floor. Her hands once again free, she held her sword of white fenneral before her, the blade shining abnormally in the peculiar light.

Sounds of lapping water soon reached their keen ears, growing in intensity until they arrived in a low-roofed cavern. The light was brightest here, highlighting everything in stomach-churning cobalt. A broken down wall, the immense stones ripped asunder as if by some terrible force, gave entrance to the sea. Other walls were cracked and full of holes big enough for a man to crawl into. Low tide. A wide pool of seawater intruded. Crabs and other sea creatures darted amongst a fantastic array of gems, priceless fenneral items and weaponry glinting from underneath a watery sheen. Decaying remains of fish and sea animals littered the floor. A long human spine sat amongst split leg bones, the marrow licked out. A pile of skulls dominated the far wall like a shrine.

The stench was almost intolerable.

Vareena covered her nose and mouth with her free hand.

A golden chain consisting of nine large interlocked links, hung upon a dripping wall. *Nine!* thought Vareena. *The number of Chicanery and arcane majiks. The same foul yellow metal rests within Scowl's evil weapons.* She shuddered.

Scowl remained impassive, sniffing at the rank air. "Golem!" he shouted, his nasal voice echoing off cold walls.

Vareena heard something stir.

"Come out, fiend," Blackbeak whispered, IronScythe firm at his side, the half-hand now holding his wicked poniard of Iron. "I am Scowl. I am on weregild to destroy you. Or are you afraid of a mere man?"

A hand, like the giant claw of the eagle, reached through a well-worn hole. Rope-like veins curled around a patchwork of roughly knitted flesh. A thick black ichor pulsed within. Talons scratched against the polished stone, twitching in time to the beat of a powerful heart.

Vareena stepped forward, pointing her sword at the creature. Only the barest quiver at the tip of her blade betrayed her fear.

"You must retreat a way," whispered Blackbeak. "This is a battle requiring iron, not stone."

"I will not stand idly by. This thing killed my father."

"So be it, but do not drop your guard."

Another vast claw appeared and the monster pulled itself through the small opening like a spider from its hole. It was man-shaped, but like no man Vareena had ever seen. The limbs were a nightmarish jumble—sharp ridges of etiolated bone pulled by ungainly muscles. Part of the creature's chest was bare of flesh, revealing the enormous ribcage of some sea animal. Within, more veins curled. What was left of the skin was a heinous mixture of man and beast raggedly stitched together like the patchwork quilt of a child. The golem dropped down from the hole to land on enlarged webbed feet, each with a wicked-looking hooked claw. A powerful shudder thumped rhythmically within the beast's shaky frame.

The abhorrence turned towards them and Vareena's stomach lurched. It possessed the head of a man but the face sagged—heavy jowls dragging its expression into that of a shrieking ghoul. A lipless mouth hung open in a perpetual, silent scream. The eyes were two empty sockets. It twitched and twisted as if trying to catch sounds from the air. *Was it blind? Could Scowl use that to his advantage?*

"Greetings," the golem hissed, crawling around the outer wall of the chamber, long claw-like fingers caressing the wet rock.

Vareena's skin crawled. *I know that voice. The same timbre as my uncle…*

"Greetings indeed," replied Scowl. "Prepare, for your doom is upon you."

The head twitched, dark pits staring right through him. "You think yourself powerful enough to kill *me?*"

"I am the destroyer of all works of delving. I have defeated stronger foes than you."

"You know nothing of me," said the twitching automaton, drooling from a mouth that did not work properly. "My life may be one of sombre woe, of emptiness and bitter pain, yet I will not let it be taken by another."

Scowl tightened his one good hand around the hilt of IronScythe.

"I can give you fortune, wealth," the creature continued, pointing to the vast array of riches that lay in abandon on the floor of the chamber. It moved closer, padding upon clawed feet. "But I sense you are not swayed by such base concerns. We are alike, you and I. More alike than you imagine."

"You attempt to jest with me, monster?"

"We are one and the same, Scowl. You were crafted from delving as surely as myself. Is that not a delving blade you wield?"

Vareena glanced at Scowl. IronScythe seemed darker under the unnatural blue light; the jagged sword cast no shadow, its edges indistinct, disturbing. Blackbeak stood still, taut like the drawstring of a powerful bow, primed and ready for combat.

"I felt your coming, my brother. I've waited many passings of the Gyre for your arrival," the golem continued.

"Then you have waited in vain. Unless you relish your own demise."

"You would kill me without listening to my tale?"

"I have little stomach for parley. Let this thing be done."

"No! You break into my house. You disturb my rest. You come here to murder me." The monster raked its claws along the stone wall. "I am this keep's master and you *will* hear me out!"

A sound that might have been a laugh emerged from Scowl's lips. "Then speak, for they shall be your last words."

The beast paused before taking breath. "The ocean has always been my home." The demon turned empty eye-sockets to the breach in the wall. "Even as a young man, I loved the invigorating touch of salty waters.

Ironic then, that the sea was the cause of my downfall. A long time ago, when I was master of Keep Krall, my captains and I held regular diving competitions to find the elusive grey oyster pearls found in open bounty upon the ocean floor. It was our manly custom to brave the depths to retrieve these prizes, for a man was measured not only by his station in life, but by the number and size of pearls worn upon his breast." The abhorrence pointed to the cavern's pool. A sizable cache of the grey pearls glowed under the water like eggs from a fabled and beautiful sea beast. The enormous frame jerked. Vareena guessed the monster was shrugging.

"Ambition and greed for success, if unchecked, can be the ruin of young men," the creature continued. "Despite my vaulted position as master, I desired the finest of all pearls. I dove deeper than the rest, searched farther afield, stayed underwater longer—none could hold their breath as long as I. But as you may guess, this ambition led to my demise. On my last dive, I went deeper than ever before and on rising to the surface, I was wracked by the most grievous pain and nearly drowned. I awoke many weeks later unable to walk or talk, a prisoner of my bed. Nothing more than a drooling invalid.

"And while I watched helplessly, all my power and influence passed to my younger brother, Dravid. I began to hate him, to despise the growing collection of pearls that he wore with open disdain upon his breast. I saw what Dravid was doing, but was powerless to stop him taking what was rightfully mine." The ghoulish head turned towards Vareena. "We Kralls are a ruthless family. By the time I recovered my tongue, it was too late. Power had shifted, my influence diminished. Dravid even stole the Krall ring, the symbol of my mastership, and made show of owning it."

Vareena glanced at her right hand and shuddered at the sight of the Ring of Souls. *I am the Mistress of Keep Krall. This flesh golem is my kin, bound to my family… to me.*

"My captains, my friends, now dived and made merry with the new master. But I still retained a few faithful vassals." The golem's claws clicked against the cold stone. "Through them I managed to secure the administrations of the best physicians. At first, my brother was worried, and I feared the touch of an assassin's blade, but as weeks passed into months, then into whole seasons with no improvement, I became an irrelevance to him. And that's how my life should have been. An invalid, shut away in one of the many towers, forgotten and useless until I died a lonely death. But as dark luck would have it, my predicament fell upon the ears… of Chicanery."

"I wondered when the evil arts of delving would enter your touching story," Scowl sneered.

"The eminent Savant-master arrived and sent all my so-called healers away. I'd known power as a younger man. In those days, I perceived my own strength in the dominion over others, getting what I wanted, when I wanted. In this man of majiks, I observed another type of potency. He appeared to be only half my age, yet was four times my span. Wisdom in the guise of a youth barely past his first gyre. He did not need the trappings of wealth or land; he did not need an army of followers or droves of lovers. No. He travelled the lands alone wearing only the simple blue weaves of Chicanery. And yet… he was so much more than any man I'd ever met. Together we set about fixing my broken body. The ambition of the Krall family burned within me. I wanted to walk again, to leave my bed and the prison of my tower, but I thirsted for more. I desired *long life*. The Savant-master promised to remake me better than before, tougher. To give me dominion over Keep Krall for countless passings of the Gyre."

"Greed is often a route to dark arts." Scowl shifted his feet with unease at the creature's slow progress towards the breached wall and escape.

The golem ignored him, seemingly lost in its story. "Delving and majiks were new then. If I'd only known his plans, I may have reconsidered what we did next. I was a blind fool. For many long months he worked his Usery upon my sad flesh. His majiks invigorated me, gave me strength and, most of all, gave me hope. Finally, I was taken under the shroud of night from my tower down into the bowels of the Keep, into this very cavern. He laid me on a stone slab, my twisted body naked and shivering. And on the slab beside me?" His claws pointed at his chest. "This foul body! Only in that moment did I realise the horror the savant-master had planned. What I'd seen as power and wisdom was nothing more than a veneer hiding madness. He was insane, sent awry by his addiction to golds and silvers."

"Metals are the downfall of all Savancery," muttered Scowl.

The brute put one clawed hand around the white sagging flesh of its chin. "The mad Savant decapitated me… I thought my life over, finished, murdered by the hands of a lunatic, yet upon my awakening—" He pointed again to his twisted body. "I found this! I would have killed him if his dark arts hadn't already stolen his life-force and invested it within me. His corpse lay upon the floor, twisted and bent in a mirror of my own. His skull, even now, rests in this cavern."

The thing of ragged flesh quivered for a second.

"This device he made of me took time to understand. I had to learn to walk again, to use my hands, to speak. Only then did I seek to enter the land of the living. A foolish notion. Look at me. What sane person would gaze at this and not run screaming? Yet I was too keen to reclaim my heritage. I left my cavern and sought out my brother. Dravid and his militia attacked me, but I soon found that no weapons of simple stone or glass could harm me. And I was so very strong. I killed Dravid and took back my place as master." It laughed. "As you may imagine, the keep folk did not take kindly to a monster's rule. I was not the man I used to be—I was no man at all. I decided to go back to my old friend the sea, leaving a grateful keep behind. I travelled north to the freezing regions where time passed less heavily under the cold shroud of ice, but I could not fully relieve my pain. What is life without companionship, people, and friends? After many passings of the Gyre, I sought out the land of Oldiva and resolved to again take up residence in Keep Krall.

"When I returned, I found another in my place; my brother's descendants. My sudden arrival appalled and sickened them. Although words of bonding were spoken, they blinded me with a blade of gold and tried to murder me. I destroyed them and, for their treachery, swore an oath to kill all descendants of Krall. This is now my home, Scowl, and it shall remain so."

"You speak well for a creature of foulness, but you have made no argument."

"Is it not clear, Scowl? We are kin. We are both reviled for our loathsome looks. Are you not also treated as a monster? Are you not attacked for no other reason than your disfigurement? Does not rancour grow in your soul with every disgusted look, every hurtful comment?"

Vareena remembered her own reaction the first time she'd seen Blackbeak and was ashamed.

"Here I can offer you a haven, a place where you will be welcome," the beast said. "A place you can return to."

Scowl kicked a small skull across the floor. It rattled amongst the other bones. "You are forgetting one thing, golem."

"And what is that, Scowl?"

"Iron!"

A thunderbolt of blue fire erupted from the golem's outstretched hands and exploded into Scowl, coruscating along IronScythe where it fizzled and burned. A sharp odour of ozone filled the air.

Blackbeak stood resolute, his eldritch blade somehow absorbing the living flame.

The fiend darted towards the breach, but the black-hooded figure jumped forward, planting himself in the brute's path. The fetid apparition stood half as high again as Scowl, yet it padded backwards, hissing from a lipless mouth. The claws came together and another thunderbolt erupted forth.

Scowl swung IronScythe, deflecting the strike into the cavern wall. An explosion of rock and masonry rained around him.

The golem dove for the golden chain hanging on the wall and lashed Blackbeak. The yellow metal seemed to have a life of its own, wrapping around IronScythe, snagging the grey, iron blade. The creature dragged Scowl within reach of its other appalling claw. Blackbeak lunged forward within the monster's grasp and thrust his wicked poniard into the attacking arm, cutting a rope-like vein. The golem howled. Black ichor dribbled. Scowl slashed again, hacking into the patchwork flesh. The arm fell twitching to the ground.

Blackbeak jerked IronScythe backwards, yanking the golden chain from the beast's grasp. The links slipped from Scowl's blade and crashed onto the floor. He took a step backward, readying a brutal swing with IronScythe, but the creature's severed arm, still full of life, grabbed at his legs and brought him tumbling down.

The monster, sensing victory, rushed at him.

"Look out!" Vareena shouted.

Blackbeak threw his poniard of iron. It thumped blade first into the fiend's chest, bubbling and burning with an unnatural smoke. Black ichor exploded from the dreadful wound. Unable to check its forward motion, the monster crashed into Scowl, desperately tugging at the poniard with its one good hand. Both rolled with the force of the impact. The severed arm flew through the air and thudded against the wall next to Vareena. She slashed at it with her sword. Despite the sharpness of her blade, the fenneral was unable to harm the weird flesh that wriggled and writhed before her.

Scowl found his feet and yelled. His sword cleaved into the golem's shoulder. Dark blood sprayed into the pool. The golem fell forwards onto its knees, desperately pulling itself towards the water and escape, its one good hand seeking the golden chain. Unperturbed, Scowl took up IronScythe in both hands and stood above the sprawling creature.

"Your Mastership is at an end, foul demon," he said, his voice distant and unconcerned. Blackbeak brought the heavy blade down and severed the monster's neck. With a deafening bang, the golem exploded in a ball of cerulean flame that sent Scowl flying. He landed with a crash.

A conflagration met Vareena's bewildered eyes as the doomed brute, its majiks broken, screamed and writhed amongst the unnatural inferno. She kicked the still twitching hand and arm into the flames and ran to Scowl. "Are you all right?"

He rubbed his leg and nodded.

Within a few minutes, nothing remained of the golem, apart from a sickly pall in the air and a molten gold puddle on the cavern floor.

Scowl stood up and retrieved his poniard—the dagger undamaged by the heat. "Come. I have fought my battle," he said as if he had just finished a training bout and not taken part in a fight that nearly saw his death. "The gauntlet has now fallen to you, Vareena."

"What do you mean?" she asked, still amazed and horrified by the demon's demise.

Scowl pointed at the pool of gold staining the floor yellow. "This room must be blocked and forever hidden."

Vareena had heard of the most perilous of all metals, but had never seen it with her own eyes. This close, gold had the power to hypnotise. "It's beautiful."

"Do not be fooled by its glister, Vareena, gold is the greatest evil."

"But does not the same metal sit within your weapons?"

His answer was a short sharp laugh. "You must seal this room and never let any enter."

"That is for my uncle Dracus to decide—isn't it?"

Scowl turned his hooded head towards her. "I am asking you, Vareena, not Dracus Krall. You are this Keep's Mistress, not him. Do you promise?"

She nodded.

"Good. Now come." He sheathed IronScythe and marched away from the cavern, leading her once again through the magnificent halls and corridors of Keep Krall.

With the golem dead, the keep didn't seem so imposing. *This is the home of my ancestors,* thought Vareena. *It belongs to me, not my uncle.* A feeling of belonging gripped her as tightly as Blackbeak grasped his dark iron.

MISTRESS VAREENA

A **HOST** awaited them beyond the bridge of stone. At least fifty armed men stood upon the far side—the Krall militia. With them, what must be the entire House of Krall. More men, women and children, and their various animals, scurried under the imposing walls of the gully. They carried high packs upon their backs. It seemed they'd come to stay. Worried faces regarded Vareena and her strange companion. At their head, stood Vareena's uncle, Dracus Krall.

Scowl moved to the bridge's edge and looked down into the sea-filled chasm as if disinterested.

Sickened eyes followed his black hood; many had been present at the Reeve and had seen the horror that lurked under his cowl.

"Brother-daughter," Dracus exclaimed. "How fare you? Is the quest done?"

The same voice as the golem! Vareena baulked. *My uncle doesn't just want Keep Krall, he seeks to topple Fangarra and make himself King-Emperor. If I let Dracus enter, I'm dead and war will come to this land.* "Our dark ancestor lies in ruin as flotsam and jetsam on the sea," she announced, drawing eyes from the gathered throng.

"At last," Dracus said and, with a resounding cheer from the House, he stepped onto the bridge.

"Keep Krall is mine, Uncle."

Dracus stopped in his tracks, worried eyes darting at Scowl.

Blackbeak turned towards him, sharp, misshapen features made visible by a blustering wind pushing at his hood. "The weregild is done; your golem is no more. I have no interest in your petty squabbles."

"Then Krall is mine." Dracus took a further step forward.

"I warn you, Uncle!"

Dracus smiled. "You were always so clever, but in some ways, just a simple child. I wondered how long it would take you to work it out. It appears you've grown up on your journey. You are like your father, whose death did not come too soon."

Vareena's head lifted to reveal two sparkling emerald eyes that spoke of anger and a renewed defiance. "I am Mistress. And you, Uncle, cannot enter."

A chuckle shook the old man's frame. "I am your elder, your clan chief. I am Dracus Krall. This keep is mine. The prophesy speaks of a King-Emperor who will arise from Krall, not a Queen. What possible claim could you have? You're nothing but a little tom-girl." He turned to the throng amassed behind him and was met with hoots and guffaws.

Ignoring the laughter, Vareena held up her hand. "This is my claim. I wear the Ring of Souls. This heirloom has passed down from first-born to first-born. Whoever wears this ring has dominion over Keep Krall. You will bow to me, Uncle. As shall all in my House."

The men stopped their sniggering. All knew of the

ring's significance.

"That is my property, girl!" Dracus lunged at her, but the whited sword of fenneral jumped into her hand, the point thrust under his throat.

Dracus' eyes narrowed. "You choose Combat?"

She nodded before she had chance to digest his words.

"Then let all here witness. Combat has been chosen. And, as is the decree of Oldivan Law, the victor shall win right to all chattels, possessions and lands of the loser." He called over the House Steward who brought him a fine-looking well-oiled fenneral sword.

Vareena turned to Scowl, but he had his back to her. *He won't help me. His fight is against delving alone. I don't need his evil blade. I have my own. If I lose to Dracus, I'll be as dead as if he kills me here and now. Scowl has at least given me that knowledge.* She took a deep breath. "I take the Death-Rite!"

"The Death-Rite?" Dracus Krall repeated in consternation.

Vareena's eyes found those of the House of Krall's Steward, Allon. "It is my right."

Allon had always been a loyal Krall man, fair and mannered in his dealings and... *handsome*. Vareena's crush on the Steward seemed far away and childish now. *I've put Allon in an impossible position. But my hands are tied.*

Dracus glared at Allon with a fiery expression.

The Steward bowed his head. "I am sorry, Master, but Law is on her side. Combat is already entered into. There is no redress."

A grim smile found Vareena's lips. *Killing me in Combat would be a crime many would not forgive, regardless of it being my choice. No, Uncle, I will not make this easy for you.*

"So be it." Dracus raised his voice. "But let all here

know that it is not my wish to kill my brother-daughter, it is she who has chosen Combat and I am Law-bound to comply. Have trust that I will do everything in my power to defeat her without blood being spilled."

"I will not submit," said Vareena, making sure everyone could hear. "If I am to die, let it be with a sword in my hand and a curse on my lips!"

A hush fell upon the gathering. The Steward stood between her and Dracus who ungirded his sword and stood in a fighter's crouch.

Allon raised his arm and backed away. *"Fight."*

Dracus leapt at her, sprightly for his age, his muscles knotted and hard. It was as Vareena had long suspected, his reliance on his staff was a feint. He was not a weak old man, far from it. He clubbed her proffered sword, once, twice, three times.

Against her will, Vareena took a step back.

Dracus laughed wickedly, changing his tack to swing the flat of his blade under her defence.

Another step back. Dracus was nimble, his sword darting, playing with her.

I cannot dodge his sword forever and I dare not attack with my own, she thought as he pushed her towards the smashed keep doors. *He is a Swordmaster!*

"You play a dangerous game, brother-daughter," Dracus whispered. "I will kill you as surely as I killed your fool father. Not now, but your time will come, that I promise."

The Ring of Souls burned hotly on her finger. Vareena squealed with pain and lunged forward, taking the old man unawares with a cut to his thigh. She took another swing and another, but Dracus quickly regained his composure, a thin sheen of sweat upon his creased brow betraying the effort.

Vareena knew she could not hold against her uncle for much longer. Desperation ate at her. The Ring of Souls singed her hand. With a yelp, she dropped her sword, the fine, white fenneral clattering on to the bridge.

A wicked smile flashed across her uncle's face. He raised his blade, holding the tip in front of her face. "And so we come to it," he said. He turned once again to the House. "Arrest her!"

Vareena clasped her hands together, squeezing out the sting from the scorching ring, turning the hurt away from herself and... *on to her uncle.*

Behind Vareena an unnatural voice bubbled. "Dracus."

The sprightly old man turned towards the sound and baulked. "—What?"

An enormous clawed hand reached over the bridge, feeling with long, grasping fingers. Another hand and then an eyeless head came into view as the phantom golem lifted itself upon the solid stone.

"No!" Dracus' face paled with abject terror.

"Yes," whispered the monster, "I've been waiting for you."

The amassed House of Krall stared at Dracus with shock and disdain. He shouted and writhed like a lunatic, waving his sword around him as if attacked by some loathsome, but invisible enemy.

Dracus whimpered as the apparition came to bear full upon the bridge. He slashed his sword, but one commanding hand ripped the fenneral from his grasp and threw the blade into the surging waters below.

"You've thought about me all your long and ambitious life, old man. Well here I am!" Arrant hands encircled the Dracus' neck and squeezed.

As the astonished crowd watched, Dracus Krall fell to his knees, shaking as if under some dreadful palsy, blood streaming from both eyeballs until, with a strangled rattle, he fell down dead.

"—Vareena."

Somewhere in the distance, a familiar voice called softly to her. "Yes," she answered from her dream.

"Keep Krall awaits you, Mistress."

She blinked. Scowl stood in front of her. "What…?" Her memory came flooding back. The pain in her hand. The Ring of Souls burning. Dracus' still twitching corpse lay on the bridge, his eyes, wide and staring. "What did I do?"

"Do not use the Ring of Souls again," whispered Scowl. "Your heirloom was crafted from delving majiks. Today you witnessed its true power. You created the illusion of the golem in Dracus' mind and it killed him."

"I understand," she whispered, rubbing her ring. She turned and faced what was now her house—the House of Keep Krall. The men and women were quiet, awe-stricken. Steward Allon stared at her with an expression of fear mixed with relief.

"Your keep awaits its new mistress," said Scowl.

Those simple words filled Vareena with strength. "Dracus Krall is dead," she said loudly with a commanding voice. "According to Law, I, Vareena Krall, claim this House as my own. If you wish to raise an objection, your time is now."

No one made a sound.

"Good. We've a lot of work to do. From this day forward, Krall will once again be a respected name in Oldiva. Kitchener, inspect your Larders—they will soon be overflowing with food. Send out the hunters and the fishers. Tonight we feast in celebration of the golem's demise, of our return to the ancestral home and to mourn the death of Dracus Krall."

The House remained quiet and leaden-footed, unsure of what to do. Steward Allon soon shouted them into some semblance of order and they began to shuffle past.

Scowl made to leave as the two hundred or so members of her House gingerly entered their new home.

"Stay with me awhile," said Vareena.

"I cannot."

"Please, there are many here who I don't trust, who don't trust me. And I do not yet know the intentions of Jhaz'Elrad."

"I am destined never to remain in one place. My next stop is Palimara. There is evil in that land. And as for the King-Emperor, with Dracus dead, I doubt he will worry about a teenage girl. Unless it is your desire to bring war to the land of Oldiva."

Vareena shook her head. "You'll stay tonight for this feast." Her lips quirked upwards. "Or I'll follow you to the ends of Arn!"

Scowl's iron-blue eyes, glimpsed behind his hood, shone with certainty "No, I leave now. Already I hear delving's call. Goodbye Vareena." He turned and strode over the bridge.

Vareena watched as the strange, dark and pained individual shrank into the distance. *Why am I so sad to see him go? Have I fallen for him… surely not?*

Steward Allon appeared at her side. "Forgive me, Mistress, but you are needed."

Vareena said nothing.

He followed her gaze. "I am grateful the golem is dead, and even more thankful that the evil creature responsible for its doom has left us."

"No, Allon," said Vareena, picking up her sword of purest white fenneral and rubbing her hand down its length. "He is a man. Maimed, broken and dangerous, maybe, but a man all the same. And let me tell you this: I would have wished him stay. Scowl will be forever welcome at Keep Krall."

WEIRDING

He was no friend of witchery, nor of the gentler majiks. Yet even he, who carried delving's doom at his side, could not resist our eldritch gramarye. A great debt we owe him, a debt still remains unpaid…

The Book of the Carline.

THE PLANES

FULMINARA'S ETHEREAL self shuddered within the Dimension Lord's powerful grasp. She would not become another member of its coterie, trapped for eternity by this hideous thing, its ugly thoughts screwing at the root of her mind. She had wandered too far, been too curious, and the creature had snapped upon her soul like a mantis upon its next meal.

"I warn you, Gibbus—you cannot keep me here forever." Fulminara, an old wizened crone, floated naked amongst a swirl of entrapping vapours, her milky green eyes defiant. "I am of the Carline, and a witch." Her voice struggled to penetrate the foggy haze.

The Dimension Lord whipped a barbed tentacle at a hovering *eydi*—a delicate, jellyfish-like creature. The lesser entity squeaked, spilling its life in a frothing mass of purple and white jelly. Gibbus offered the remains to its captive.

Fulminara declined with an angry wave of her bony fingers.

Gibbus was a spectrum beast, *a colour-god*. Its bloated body, a blob of translucent flesh upon which many hues sprayed forth, flushed mauve. A slight rebuke. Nothing more than a shrug of the shoulders in a human. It held the twitching *eydi* over an array of flapping pouches gaping in obscene competition from its midriff. A scene reminiscent of a morsel presented to so many hungry beaks. It chose and the *eydi* was engulfed.

Behind the colour-god, the Morassic Seas churned a dull red, while above the beach, fat brown clouds sucked at thinner yellow vapours.

Fulminara had been dream-walking—drifting through the planes in search of… she knew not what. But to be Carline was to be curious. And Fulminara was queen amongst them. The colour-god's mind had snared her Inner—what some called a soul—and she was powerless in the creature's practiced grasp. "Set me free!"

I have made the Plane of Realities my domain, for all dimensions cross and are real at this point. Here I wait. Here I entrap unwary visitors, for all travellers are attracted to this place. You shall be the next member of my Hive, and my strength can only grow.

"No."

I feel the power of your refusal, but you are master of only one. With every passing moment, my hold grows. Soon it shall be impossible for you to escape my clutches. You are old and weak.

Fulminara regarded the colour-god with sunken eyes. "What do you know of age? The passing of simple time is no concern to one such as I." She coated her words with defiance, yet here, in this dimension, she felt exposed. She could not hide behind her most basic of witchery. Her head twitched with impotent fury.

Gibbus' thirty-six stalked, bobbing eyes looked straight through her. *The dimensions are infinite, as you well know. My power as lord comes from my mastery in two hundred and seventeen planes. To gain that mastery, I take a familiar from each.*

The colour-god swept a single tentacle in a commanding arc. Revealed in the thick air—a vast array of shadowy creatures of outlandish design.

This is my Hive. These are my familiars.

Amorphous shapes danced in front of Fulminara; lumps quivered, spines twitched, scales and feathers flapped—a hideous display. A total contrast to the Plane of Realities, a beautiful, serene place of gentle, living clouds and delicate creatures. Another wave of the barbed tentacle and Gibbus' Hive disappeared.

Fulminara's next move was desperate, but as often is the way with the Carline, words came unbidden to her mind, flowing as easily as her enchantments. "Gibbus, all dimensions have different harmonies and balances. In my world, and many others, such matters are decided by contest."

'Contest?' I have never heard of such a thing.

"A creature chosen from your dimension set in combat against a creature from mine. One fighting for Lord Gibbus, the other on my behalf."

The colour-god glowed deep blue.

"If your champion prevails, I shall gladly yield. If my champion is the victor, you shall release me and bother my dimension no more."

Blue flashed to grey contemplation. *A curious notion in which I give up the certainty of your servitude for a half chance of losing it... the idea has a certain merit. A lighter,* more cautious blue of excitement flushed the colour-god's extremities. *So be it, witch.*

Leathery tentacles whipped at a materializing eydi, scything through its air bag. It burst incandescent purple and floated limply in the air. The pouches along Gibbus' belly began to chatter. *Go, find your champion. But remember, I still hold your Inner, and can squeeze at will.*

Fulminara bowed graciously.

Drifting back to her own dimension, to her corporeal self, the reality of her situation hit as hard as a falling boulder of cold obsidian. She was of the Carline—a witch, and such witchery relied heavily upon fate. It alone would decide this contest. She gave herself wholly to it, and with abandon.

BEAVERS

A LARGE, paddle-like tail knocked Scowl aside as if he was made of straw. Sharp incisor teeth snapped together in a repeated click as a mammoth head—all jaws and beady eyes—lunged towards him. Scowl found his feet, jumping backwards out of reach of the deadly bite.

The giant beaver was a territorial animal, fierce and angry. He had mistakenly entered its snow-covered den on the side of a rocky ravine. The beast had dammed the mountain stream in its upper reaches, too high for any such creature—or so he'd thought. The blizzard that forced him into what seemed like a welcoming cave also hid its spoor. Scowl was awoken by the curious animal sniffing him, and although he had quickly vacated its hideout, the beaver had given chase.

The beast lunged at him.

Don't make me unsheathe IronScythe.

He rolled forward, his one good hand finding a hefty branch, both ends chewed by powerful teeth. The beaver pounced, knocking the wood from his grasp, bleating with a peculiar high-pitched whine, its flat nostrils opening and closing. The animal did not push its attack. It seemed wary of the intruder.

Scowl scrambled away from those sharp teeth, finding his feet and IronScythe. A giant head, twice as big as the younger, smaller beaver, emerged from underneath a snowdrift-covered opening. The creature struggled against the prison of snow with a deeper, more threatening sound.

"I truly am sorry," Scowl said quietly. He sprinted to where the beast thrashed and, in one clean strike of the iron blade, removed half its head. Skull and brains splashed on the snow.

The youngster came straight at him. IronScythe stabbed it through. The stricken creature squealed and died.

More growling and the pad of heavy paws.

Scowl darted upwards. Past the beavers' cave-like den and their frozen pool, climbing the snow-filled ravine. Jumping from rock to rock skirting the icy stream. Retreat was not his normal style, but the beasts did not deserve to die so pointlessly at the hand of the She-blade. Only the occasional clack of claw upon stone betrayed their pursuit.

After a tough climb, the land opened out and he was able to run. He ascended with speed, his clumsy hood blown into his sharp nose, his bare chin and lips limned with ice. Blackbeak's pole-like legs ate up the distance, yet four of the creatures still gave pursuit, scrambling across the frozen snow covered surface.

He reached a flinty ridge stretching in either direction. Here, the rock was glass-like and melted, crunching under his feet. Slowing his pace, he barely stopped himself from falling. He stood, wobbling on the lip of an enormous crater—staring down at a circular depression in the land that stretched for leagues. A thick, black forest sat at its centre, huddling around a spire of truncated rock jutting up like an impudent thumb.

No time for contemplation. The beavers arrived as one. Again, IronScythe found his hand and he was unable to prevent her wrath. She sliced the front paws off the lead animal with one swing and stabbed with another. A young individual leapt at him. Scowl sidestepped and the creature plunged shrieking into the abyss. Two more remained. Blackbeak ran at them, flicking his sword in and out like a serpent's tongue. Both fell to the arcane blade. The melee was over almost before it had started.

He regarded the bloodied corpses with disdain. Twin, iron-blue intent eyes flashed from behind the rough tears in his hood. *Fine-looking, proud animals—and pride always leads to a fall.*

Blackbeak was travelling through the northern ranges of Oldiva, towards Palimara—a once beautiful kingdom, if fables could be believed. Mining for fenneral, the weapon stone, had riddled the land with holes and vast ugly quarries. In comparison, Northern Oldiva was a bleak landscape of wide plains and rocky mounts plagued by winds and windblown ice. A land far too easy to become lost within.

If I am indeed lost—which I doubt. The She-blade brought me here. That much is certain. Yet no delving lurks inside this crater and its stunted spire. I'd feel it.

Eltirren, the Sun's cold sister, glinted low on the horizon. The short night would soon arrive accompanied, as ever, by a biting wind. Quickly skinning one of the dead beavers to use its pelt as a blanket, Scowl found a rocky hollow and let sleep take him.

LOVERS

WIND WHISTLED through the high ramparts of Keep Krall. A cold, Bluster's night. One of many Vareena had spent lying warm in her bed, curled up within the strong arms of Allon, the Krall family's loyal steward. Snug underneath rich furs, a dung fire burning in the hearth. But tonight, all was not well between them and Vareena found it impossible to sleep.

Older than herself by nearly two passings of the Gyre, stoic and hardworking, Allon's attentions were as surprising as her own matching desire. Soon after Vareena reclaimed what was rightfully hers, the magnificent Keep Krall, a change came over him. He softened. And a smile was sooner to find his lips. They worked closely together. Him practical, assured and respected by the House. Her full of energy, drive and creativity.

Vareena was barely out of adolescence and, although not shy or unaware of the ways of men and women, she'd never taken a lover. Boys her own age were just that—*boys*. Older men had been frightened of her now dead Uncle Dracus or put off by her warrior weaves and tomboyish antics.

Late one night, six months ago, Allon turned up at her quarters—drunk. Having secretly liked him from afar, she knew he was no drinker. His pass, when it came, was awkward and embarrassing. He'd pulled her onto the bed where he promptly passed out. *But the next morning…*

Vareena smiled at the memory. A most eventful time. When not learning the ways of love, she was busy in her new role of Mistress Krall. The Keep possessed many levels, numerous rooms and a whole multitude of corridors and stairs. The task to make them habitable was immense and not without its difficulties. Not everyone in the House had accepted her authority so readily.

If not for Allon, this transition would have been impossible. He gave the example of respect that the rest had followed. Tall, healthy, well-built and sure, Allon typified his job better than any other. He had gained his position by hard work and worth—was in his prime—and relished his role as steward with an arrogance his Mistress found amusing. Often she would stare with unrestrained pride when he solved disputes or ordered her vassals and drudges. He could almost have been the master. His face was impassive, crowned by a head of short-cropped prematurely greying black hair, giving him a natural authority that was beyond his seasons.

In the months since she became Mistress, many chattel wagons, drawn by tired looking drudges, arrived at the magnificent new doors of her island citadel. Ships sailed up the coast bringing with them furniture and fresh weavery. All manner of things wended their way across the sea from the greater civilisation of the South.

Soon Keep Krall had raiment to match its majesty.

The vast underground vault where the golem of flesh—her vile ancestor—once lived was out of bounds to everyone except Vareena and Allon. No such decree was needed. The monster that had lurked there for generation upon generation still weighed heavily in everyone's minds. None would enter those foreboding vaults.

Down in what used to be the golem's lair was an enormous cache of wealth to outshine King-Emperor Jhaz'Elrad himself. But riches were not everything. The harsh blizzards of Bluster and the many months of the snow-locked season of Tranquillity were soon to assail the land. If her House was to survive, it needed a sizeable levy to feed all those hungry mouths. Normally a Keep relied on a host of levyer villages whose inhabitants brought a tithe of food to be stored in the good seasons in return for shelter during the bad. The underground larders would slowly fill and the boundless stash of provisions shared amongst all. *The levy.*

But now there were no villages, and more importantly, no food in the larders. And so, at vast expense, Vareena paid for the rations herself.

A short distance down the coastline lay a large harbour behind which ruined buildings poked and jutted. Before the golem, the marina had been a thriving fishing town. Such deterioration sat uneasily upon Vareena. She hated its broken dwellings and resolved to make the port her first levying village. With time running out before the snows came proper, she paid for carvers and masons to start repairs. They rebuilt the quayside, replaced groynes and dredged the harbour. She travelled to the capital city of Fangarra and spread word that, for those willing to work, a good living was to be had serving the larders of Keep Krall. She ordered a brand new fishing fleet, buying ships from the Unbidden Isles and the clusters of communities that dotted the coast. Soon, the Grievery, the crafting-house in charge of the levy, was salting a fresh supply of various sea-foods. The smell of fish sizzling in herbs and garlic suffused the keep with promises of full stomachs and good provender.

All had gone well—until the last few weeks. And was the reason why she could not sleep. Allon had changed. He denied it, but their easy relationship had become strained. His attention was elsewhere. Like tonight. She had made her intentions very clear, or so she thought. And yet, after a brief hug, he had settled down to sleep.

She poked him.

Allon's eyes flicked open. "Still awake?"

Vareena wriggled out of his arms and sat up, the furs falling from her naked body. "I would sleep better if you did your duty for your mistress."

She had seen his poker face many times, in his dealings with the keep's men, women, and the flurry of merchants now eager to open trade and caravan routes. His inscrutability was admirable, but she preferred to not be on the receiving end. She was not one for secrets and intrigue—words and emotions spilled from her like a mountain stream.

"I'm tired. You also need your sleep," he said.

"I know what I want, and it's not sleep. Are you… bored with me already?"

The barest twitch of his head as if the question did not merit an answer.

"I may let you be master in the bedroom, but never forget I am your Queen."

"Don't be angry. It's been a long day and your faithful steward is not as young as he was."

"Or you tired yourself out with all those kitchen vassals. The larders are a fine place for dalliances and you must know how they swoon over you."

"I have eyes only for my Mistress."

"It's not your eyes I'm interested in."

Allon pushed back a cured bed-fur with irritation, revealing his barrel chest. Thick hair curled all the way from his waist to his collarbones. His hand rubbed uncharacteristically at the lines furrowing his brow. "Go to sleep, V'reen," he ordered.

"I don't care if you have other lovers," she said, tilting her chin up. *I am hardly ready to settle down with the first man to come along*. "As long as you're discreet, you can do what you want. I put no constrains on you. You do not have to share my bed."

"It is not I who am causing tongues to wag. Your transformation from girl to womanhood is plain for all to see."

"They may suspect something, but I am the Mistress and can take courtesans as and when I please. Let them say otherwise."

"None would dare."

"Whatever happens between us, nothing will change. You will still have my respect. You will always be my faithful steward. You understand that, yes?"

A crack in Allon's inscrutability—a momentary flash of guilt.

"You're hiding something?"

Allon reached out to her with thick, muscular arms. "Nothing. Come here."

Vareena pushed him away. "You're lying. It's in your eyes. What the Gyre is going on with you. You've not been yourself for weeks. What are you hiding from me?"

"Sleep. We'll talk about this in the morning."

From somewhere in the corridor below her quarters, Vareena heard the sudden clatter of sword upon sword and the shouts of men. "Wha—?"

Allon cursed. "Idiots! I told them to wait for my sign."

Swords meant only one thing. Treason. Vareena leapt out of bed, searching for her blade of purest white fenneral. "You're betraying me? You?"

"I did what had to be done. I'm sorry, Vareena. Truly sorry. Things would've been much simpler if you'd gone to sleep. But you're a stubborn sort. And King Emperor Jhaz'Elrad's forces have little patience. They now storm your keep. You wondered why I was tired today… I have been busy making sure they will not face much opposition. The few guards, the odd vassal… They are being taken care of."

Where is my damn sword! "But I thought—"

"That I cared you? For your many wits, you are such a child. There is no place for emotion when playing the game. It's unfortunate that you have to die, but at least you'll die a woman. I made sure of that.

"Allon, you fool."

"It is you who have been foolish. Did you think Jhaz'Elrad would sit idly by whilst you built a secret army to topple him?"

"What are you talking about?"

"The death of Dracus stayed the King's hand but I convinced him you were still a threat. All know of the Krall family's ambition. I befriended Jhaz's spy and spun him such a tale. You made it easy. Travelling to Fangarra, showing off your 'great wealth' and out-bidding his prized merchants. This Keep will soon belong to the King-Emperor and I will rule in his name."

Vareena Krall pulled herself to full height. "And are

you to be my executioner?"

Allon got out of bed, his hand around the hilt of her missing blade. "I think you're looking for this." He raised the blade threateningly. "What must be done, must be done."

The sounds of fighting abruptly stopped. The stomp and thud of heavy boots approached the closed doors to their quarters.

"I may be a child in your eyes, but even I can see you have been played. Do you really think the king will let you live?"

Momentary doubt passed over his face. "I'll take my chances."

Vareena stood lithe, naked and defiant. Lank brown-blonde hair hung upon her muscled shoulders, her skin glistening red in the embers from the fire.

Allon's eyes flickered over her body. "You're a fine specimen of a woman, but the Krall line must end." He opened his palm to reveal the Ring of Souls. "This ring of yours will soon belong to Jhaz'Elrad and with it, dominion over Keep Krall. This is what I'll use to buy my life, should I need to."

"I never did tell you what happened to Dracus Krall, did I?"

"Why speak of that fool? He went mad. Died before my eyes."

"No, Steward Allon. I killed him. Scowl once told me that I hardly touched the power of my ring. He was right. *I don't even need to be wearing it…*"

The air around Vareena shimmered and she disappeared.

Before Allon could utter an astonished word, a large earthen pot leapt from the hearth and hit him squarely in the face, shattering. He crumpled, the sword clattering to the floor. The ring fell from his grasp, rolling across old floorboards and down a gap between them.

"No!" Vareena shouted, flickering back into view.

The doors burst open and four militiamen, all wearing the garb of Jhaz'Elrad, rushed inside. Their swords bloody, their faces grim. Vareena was shocked to recognise Captain Shyk.

"Kill him, Captain!" she shouted, pointing to Allon who lay half-unconscious on his back, a red, bleeding gash halfway across his face.

Shyk stared at Allon and the naked noble girl. A smile crawled up from his mouth to turn into a leer. "You cannot fool old Shyk so easily, girl. And they say the Gyre is a harsh mistress. Seems she's decided to give me a reward at last. Bar the doors, lads, we are going to have some fun!" he threw down his blade and began to undo his breeches.

Vareena dove for her sword, rolling to land in a fighter's crouch. The tip of her blade jutting at the men. She assessed them quickly. *Captain Shyk is the veteran, and his men? Just boys.* They bore scratches and minor wounds, and did not expect or want another fight. *I have practiced long and hard since my contest with Dracus. They do not know how dangerous I am…*

"Now, now, Vareena." Shyk raised his hands. "This will go a lot easier for you if you don't put up a—"

Vareena launched herself at him, stabbing the rat-like captain in the throat. A geyser of crimson spewed forth, bathing her flesh in red and blinding the other men. She dispatched them like a practiced butcher in an abattoir.

More shouts from outside. Vareena closed the doors and barricaded them with what furniture she could find.

It won't hold long. Hopefully—just long enough.

Wiping Shyk's blood from her naked body, Vareena went to her wardrobe and donned her old fighting weaves, stuffing a bag of gems and jewellery inside the tight leather. More militia arrived at her rooms and attempted to batter down the doors. Vareena crouched above the ancient floorboards, but couldn't locate her ring.

Damn it!

Behind her, Allon groaned. She glared at him. "You stupid, ambitious fool. I'll let Jhaz'Elrad deal with you. You deserve no better than his gibbet."

She quickly pulled on one of the dead soldier's over-weaves. Bloody, with her hair tied under a leather cap and clutching at her white fenneral sword, she was almost unrecognisable. Vareena opened an oaken panel hidden behind a thick wall-hanging. A secret way out of her rooms that even Allon didn't know of.

She stole through, closing the concealed door behind her and headed to the Larders.

I cannot win this fight alone. I need food and provisions if I'm to leave here and survive the cold seasons. I hate to abandon Keep Krall, but tonight isn't the time for revenge. No. I must follow Scowl to Palimara. I'll buy a real army, one that can topple Jhaz'Elrad—The Krall name will live on. I vow it.

COME...

MANY DAYS passed while Scowl tried to find a way down into the crater. The walls were steep, treacherous and covered in scree. Loose boulders threatened avalanches, and overhangs were apt to fall at the barest disturbance. His search was finally rewarded when he spied a herd of mountain goats. He followed their well-worn tracks down to the basin floor and feasted on their cooked flesh.

The journey towards the black forest and its peculiar, thumb-like spire took weeks longer than he'd expected. Distances were deceptive in this vast crater.

As he got closer, Scowl spotted crows—thousands of them—circling the spire's stunted upper reaches like vultures around a corpse.

Too many birds. Especially for this late in the season. When they did flock together, which was rare, it was known as a 'murder of crows'—this was more like a massacre.

The forest borders were an odd place. Shadows danced under boughs twisted awry by some perverse artistry of the wind. The trees, which had lost their four-season covering of green, were already beginning to furl up, buttressing themselves against the heavy falls of snow that would keep them covered for over fifteen months. Their timbers were black and hard. Long branches twisted as if in pain. Others hung limply, filigreed boughs caressing the earth with etiolated fingers. He'd seen many such places before, yet this forest unsettled him.

Through the jagged holes cut into his hood, it appeared the trees were swaying to some unheard, lilting rhythm.

No delving lives here, that much is sure. And trees are no match for IronScythe.

He'd dealt many blows against delving, but here in this forest-place, was something outside his ken. He removed his cowl—the hood that hid his obscenity of a face. It only served to hinder him in the dark.

A flutter of wings and hundreds of crows, their feathers glistening in the light of the sun, descended from above, surrounding him. Black plumage, feet, beaks, and beady, black eyes. They squawked and cawed, perching in trees, and hopping on the uneven forest floor. *Caw caw caw!*

Scowl eyed them with suspicion. These birds were only ever seen together on battlefields. Unwelcome carrion feeders. A sign of death in any land. He regarded them for long moments, but they did nothing but stare back.

"Be gone!" he shouted, kicking at the birds, but they easily sidestepped him.

Turning his back on their derisive calls, he walked into the forest. Tall and intent, his sable weavery crowned by a mop of long, bushy, raven-coloured hair, Scowl blended into the growing dusk as if he belonged there. A crushed beak of a nose sniffed the shadows while close set iron-blue eyes narrowed.

He paused. The woodland was an ebon place and although Scowl had naturally aided sight at night, he could not pierce the murk.

'Bah!' he called into the forest gloom and strode forward. Too soon, his bravado was put to the test. The wood murmured in the darkness. When he stopped, there was only the wind in his ears. When he moved, a horde of bleary devils seemed to whisper his doom.

The hisses, creaks and groans grew in volume and rhythm. An unnatural cadence. A living, breathing voice: *Come Scowl...*

"Show yourself!" Blackbeak barked, but the wood swallowed his words. *Am I hearing things?*

Boughs and twigs brushed against him. A large branch shifted, blocking his way. A mighty swing and IronScythe bit into the hard black wood. Again he chopped, hacking with the full weight of a weapon that could fell medium-sized trees with one stroke. A long tree limb whipped at his face. Another branch stabbed his thighs. He brought the flat blade of IronScythe down, splintering the wood—her weight alone snapping the tough sinews.

The She-scythe passed through these crawling limbs with defiant strength. He grunted and yelled, hacked and sliced. To no avail. Where one bough was cut, another was sure to replace it. They hemmed him in on all sides—apart from one. He had no choice but to let himself be corralled.

The living wood pushed and pressed him for what felt like many days. He slept whenever he could, but not for long. The forest did not want him to rest. And always, the same outlandish whispering voice: *Come Scowl...*

Come. Blackbeak wondered if this was to be his fate, to die within this tree-ridden darkness. *IronScythe has always guided me true. She will not let me down. She must have good reason to bring me here to this forest.*

Scowl was lost in a well of shadows, a madman screaming at the intractable black. And when he thought he could no longer endure the oppressive forest night, something glinted in the distance. *Sunlight!*

He stumbled forward into a clearing, his half-hand shielding his eyes until he found stone—the central thumb-like spire of the crater. Rough steps led upwards and, as if urged on by some unknown force, he took them two at a time, laughing with the hysteria of escape and bathing in the cold sunlight like it was a hot summer's day. He ascended with speed, spiralling around the peculiar outcrop. A wave of sound fell upon him—the flap of countless wings—the crows returning, cawing loudly. Excited. Scowl batted them aside like so many bloated flies.

Come Scowl...

Atop the truncated spire was another forest. A dense ring of trees with bark the colour of silver, festooned with thick-stemmed, choking ivy. Like silent, gaudily dressed warriors. Where below the trees were dark and threatening, the forest here had a lighter aspect and an abundant covering of green. Leaves rustled and whispered in a constant breeze.

The crows flocked again, spinning in dizzying circles of black bodies. He ran through the hoary woodland, heading inwards until he found a pillar of rock painted with odd symbols and glyphs in reds and blues. The forest bowed towards this lith-stone, seemingly in supplication. A jumble of dry and twisted branches sat at its base.

Some kind of sacrificial pyre?

A hiss like a serpent: "Come."

The voice was no longer a whisper amongst the trees; the sound came from a human mouth, leathery and dry—the croak of an old woman. Blackbeak unsheathed IronScythe, coming back to himself. "Who is there? Show yourself, or I will fell your forest and put it to the torch!"

A sudden movement at the base of the lith, and the twisted branches came to life.

Unfurling.

Untwisting.

Scowl leapt backwards in alarm. This was no pyre, but the limbs of a dried out corpse.

The hissing turned into words. Archaic, strangled words. A strange cant that slithered through the copse like a serpent. "Come with me, Scowl. Come."

The corpse-like figure found its feet and stood naked before him. An old wizened crone. The ruin of a woman. Her flesh was more bark than skin, sagging from an emaciated frame. Her eyes were dead, long-forgotten things.

"What manner of evil are you?"

A sound that wanted to be a laugh escaped from her dry lips. She raised her hands to form a bony union above her head.

A large crow crashed into her trembling chest, knocking her to the ground. Sticking against her. Trapped. Then another. The birds were somehow consumed, their flesh absorbed, leaving only feathers and dry bones behind. The tiny glade filled with a flurry of beating black wings, hundreds of crows cawing in distress and panic, drawn to the female demon lying before him.

Scowl stared until the shrieks and caws stopped. The crone lay under a vast mound of dead, broken corpses.

With a giggle, the pile was pushed aside to reveal a striking, pale-skinned woman. Her hair was as red as the sun on the hottest day of Blaze and her eyes the deepest green he had ever seen. A handsome and beguiling demoness. The crone reborn as a lush naked woman. She stood on long legs, stretching with feline grace. "Take him—"

Thick ivy found Scowl's wrist, knitting around his arm and IronScythe. He reached for his poniard with his half-hand, but it was knocked aside and ensnared by a vicious branch. More ivy and roots entangled his feet. A sinuous bough encircled his waist, and he was jerked towards the lith-stone like a virgin to a sacrifice. He was trapped, and at the mercy of this forest devil.

The woman's hands caressed the milk-white skin of her belly, sliding upwards to cup her now full breasts, each capped with a cherry-coloured nipple. A thick triangle of red pubic hair curled invitingly. Lips curved into a smile, revealing a muscular tongue licking at a set of perfect teeth. A well-proportioned beauty.

Too beautiful. False.

"You ask what I am? I am loveliness. I am desire—I am many things. Fulminara is my name. I am Carline and witch." She swaggered up to him. "You do well to keep such a face hidden."

"The last face you'll ever see, witch."

"I think not. Blackbeak is the nemesis of delving not witchery. We both share hatred of those arts, and of Chicanery. Besides, we Carline are not easily killed." She waved a single hand towards the pile of dead crows and smiled again. "New flesh can always be found."

"You are... *Carline?*"

She ran fingers through her voluminous hair. "Red-orange locks betray the weirding as a one-handed beggar betrays the thief. Yes, I am Carline. What you heard as whispers in the woods was my *gramarye*, my *weirding*." Her reborn voice thrilled the air. The words were low, subtle and rose and fell like a playful breeze through a summer forest canopy.

Scowl tried to shake his head. "The Carline belonged to a dead age. They are gone. Forgotten. Just how long have you lain here?"

A frown played over the beautiful woman's face. "I have waited many lifetimes for your coming, sustained by the Planes—maybe longer than I realised."

"What do you want with me?"

"Want? Do you not yet understand? You are mine, Scowl. To do my bidding as I wish."

"I follow no command but IronScythe!"

The emerald eyes widened. From her throat came a soothing sound. The branch around Scowl's neck tightened.

Blackbeak choked and spluttered while she enjoyed the spectacle.

"The strangled gasp, the sigh, the delicate moan, how they pleasure. I could live for a thousand passings of the Gyre upon their shuddering waves of ecstasy. How close they are—love and death. But worry not. I will not snuff out what is so dear, so priceless—*so unique*."

With a wave of her hand, she released the branch's grip.

He took a pained breath. "You know what I am?"

"We Carline have the gift of *Sight*. I know who you *are, and that you are not from this world*. Yet there is much in you that is hidden. 'Tis strange that for my own ends I should employ an avenger of the opposite arts." Her eyes dropped to IronScythe.

"'Opposite arts?'"

"Yes. For I perceive the power of Chicanery in your iron." Her lip curled. "I detest everything connected with Cairn and its malingering coterie. The majiks? Bah! We Carline witnessed first-hand the destruction they caused to our world of Arn. The Usery and all its fat savants are tied too close to Arn's power. They feed off its raw energy, its life-blood. Leeches they are, parasites!"

"You're no different, despite your pretensions. The majiks flow through you like any other savant or user."

"'Tis true that we Carline are likewise connected to Arn, but we are the natural enemies of Chicanery; for where the majiks burn and incinerate with awesome power, weirding soothes and persuades; explores and experiences. Is it evil? No. Nor foul or unwholesome. Weirding represents a gentler force; something in touch with nature, that has a certain control over it. We hurt nothing that cannot be replenished. Like those crows who gladly gave their flesh to resurrect my own. Weirding is a celebration of life and its urges, of love itself, of death and desire—of the natural order. All that the majiks are not."

"I too hate the majiks and will have nothing to do with them."

"Fool. You are them!" she scoffed and stepped closer, her face inches from Scowl. "Can't you see that? I did not take you for an idiot."

He spat at her, the close-set, iron-blue eyes defiant.

She wiped the spittle with one long-nailed finger and licked at it with a glistening tongue. "You have a certain sordid fascination." Her eyes flicked across Scowl's broken face—hot breath caressing his exposed cheek. "I took a vow to kill all Chicanery, to destroy those greedy men of power as they once sought to destroy all Carline. But men have their uses. As long as they know their place."

Her hand found his inner thigh. Sharp nails dug at him. A smell of womanliness, of secure warmth and hidden excitements, enticed. Scowl turned his head away.

"You are a strange one, but a man all the same. If I'm saved, we will have plenty of time for desire."

"End your riddles, witch."

Fulminara pulled away, shouting to the sky. "I have found my champion at last!" And then, in a whisper, she continued. "Let us hope your opponent doesn't defeat you as easily as I." Fulminara giggled into the forest, her laugh carried upon the wind to rise above the trees in a deafening squeal that crowded all other sounds—

Come.

Scowl shivered at the timbre of this word, spoken somewhere outside of reality.

Come Scowl—Come with me—Walk with me—Fly with me.

A sharp tingling worried at the base of Blackbeak's spine, spreading throughout his frame. He tensed; the sensation existed just on the edge of pain.

I want you—I need you—What kind of love is in you?— Come to Me—Feel Me—Touch Me—Love Me…

Scowl struggled against his living bonds. They held him fast; and yet, such was the nature of Fulminara's gramarye that he wanted to let those words swallow him up.

Let your spirit fly—Come float up high—Fly the planes— Ignore your pains—Come with Me fly—Hear their roar—Let yourself soar.

The weirding had him now; her wording reached the back of his skull with soft velvet fingers and caressed his brain. Teasing, pulling, tempting. Her eyes filled his vision—great green orbs of scintillating light blotting out all except her insistent gaze.

You want Me—You need Me—You want to fly free—Ah yes—I feel your smile—Come—Bring your essence—Leave awhile—Release your body—Free your mind—Leave this world far behind.

Scowl could not resist.

Come Scowl—Take my hand—Touch my flesh—Leave this land.

The trees faded, leaving only two wide green eyes blazing into his soul.

A new voice muttered somewhere upon the wind— *Yes.*

LOST

VAREENA AWOKE choking. A force held her head, covered her nose and mouth, pinching in a dreadful grasp that tried to smother her. She screamed somewhere inside only to find it was her own hands covering her face. Shocked and appalled by the dream, and desperate to breathe, she untied the tent's flap and pushed out into the freezing night. A cold blast of air brought her back to full consciousness.

How many more nights will I suffer these insidious dreams?

Weeks had passed since she had escaped Keep Krall. Eastwards had seemed the only option—the road to Fangarra and the South would be watched. Yet she had not realised how far she had to travel alone in the wilderness before reaching civilisation. And she had another problem. She was lost.

She travelled *The Salted Wastes*. An immense flat land reclaimed from the seas in Gyre's past. An overpowering austerity possessed it—bleaker than usual for this region. Vareena had navigated by the sun on a clear north-easterly course to Palimara, but the expected outer towns and villages skirting the rough land known as *The Grikes* had yet to appear. The Wastes seemed to stretch on forever.

She made a quick meal of berries and the last of her dried fish and packed her tent. Necessity had caused her to steal the dead militiaman's over-weave back in her chambers, but she was ever thankful for it. Jhaz'Elrad might be showy, yet his ostentation was reflected in the fur-lined, elaborate uniforms of his militia. The overcoat was snug and warm. She pulled the heavy garment around her shoulders and shivered.

She may no longer be Mistress of Keep Krall, yet Vareena enjoyed this solitary time—despite her feelings of loss. Her life had been one headlong dash forward—but to what end? Within months, she had changed from tom-girl to Queen and had taken her first lover. Now, as the long days passed, she had all the time in the world. *Let Jhaz'Elrad think me gone and forgotten, and when he least expects it, I'll return triumphant.*

A thin snow had been falling ever since she started this journey. The cold she could endure—although the blizzards proper could arrive at any time. At least food was easy to find when tracks were so easy to follow. *But the road remains hidden. Maybe I've come too far north?*

Only her anger and determination had kept her on this path.

Vareena was no fool. Her schooling had been as wide as it had been boring. She knew how to navigate by sun and star, but after following the same direction for all this time without any sign of civilisation, the possibility arose that she may die out here. Weeks came and went, and with them, the niggling feeling she must turn south or perish. Her self-belief told her the land of Palimara was close by, yet some other part of her, something instinctive, said otherwise. One thing was for sure—if she went southwards far enough she'd find Ariva and the sea, and from there she could get her bearings.

Palimara may be a day away, yet I cannot take the chance. South it must be.

But the decision irked. Why? Vareena knew the answer. Some part of her was following Scowl, hoping to meet up with him again. A bond had developed during their adventure to kill the golem and, although she longed to return to Keep Krall to reclaim what was rightfully hers, she could not get the enigmatic warrior out of her thoughts. *He's a boy, my age. Crushed by unfortunate deformities and forced to carry a blade marking him as dangerous and untrustworthy. How awful to wander the lands alone under such a dreadful curse. After so many months, he'll be long gone. Won't he?*

She remembered Allon's touch, their lovemaking. Her youthful, exuberant desire; giving herself to him. *Do I want the same from Scowl? Is that it? Do I want to be in his arms?* She imagined the caress of his half-hand against her naked skin, his long black hair brushing the back of her neck—and IronScythe held in his other hand. *He's nothing without his blade and I'd not allow such an evil thing into my bedchamber. These thoughts are ridiculous, stupid… and yet? I'd trust my soul to him more than any other. He'd never betray me, although I guess his heart is made of stone.*

Some said travelling south was easier because you walked 'downhill', and as soon as she packed her tent and pointed her feet southwards, her backpack and her mood became lighter.

An hour later, walking across the windswept plain, she had the sensation of being watched. She turned, spotting a dark cloud on the northern horizon, a haze of grey in the early morning cerulean sky. It came closer, until she realised it was made from thousands of tiny black shapes.

Birds.

This was the season of Tempest, also known as Bluster. No animals migrated to warmer climes—*where'd they go when all lands froze?* Like most creatures, except man and his domestic animals, they sought the slumber of under-earth, deep in the ground, or in hidden caverns and cracks. *In this season, most birds would still be on the wing, not flying together. Only when the heavy snow came would they disappear from the skies.*

Vareena did not fear them, yet something was amiss. Whatever the flock's purpose, she had nowhere to hide.

CHAMPIONS

THIS IS *your advocate?* Gibbus glowed a sarcastic orange. His thirty-six eyes, each atop a long stalk, caressed the air before the crouched, naked figure crowned with a thick mop of black hair. They bobbed in a mimicry of derision.

"Aye, Gibbus. This is my champion."

Scowl opened his eyes. A vista beyond his wildest imaginings. He sat beside a reddened sea. Its sluggish waves, like thick treacle, crawled up a long blue beach to crash in listless, foaming silence. The horizon twisted as if viewed through a moving spyglass, and the air was a cloying veil upon which floated strange creatures of many shapes and sizes, reminiscent of swimming jellyfish. High above, living clouds of yellow protoplasm, drifted lazily. There was no sound, apart from a keening, high-pitched wail. Like a nightmare made from over-indulgence of dream-hemp or hyyrh-weed.

Scowl had addled his mind on many occasions, partaken of narcotics and opiates in the hills of Domarland bordering the Dominion of Cairn and its city of majiks, and spent lengthy befuddled months in the gloomy dens of the Unbidden Isles. There he had dwelled longer than he had intended. The Isles were full of pirates, bootleggers and low-lifes of all kinds.

Blackbeak's dark countenance had fit in well with such folk who did not question or pry. He passed his time mostly alone, ignoring IronScythe's insistent pull. Cerrut was in abundance and also gula bark—the black, mind-altering wood chewed by many late into the night. This intense period of indulgence had pushed his inner pain far away, leaving him dead-eyed and lifeless. It was the only way he could escape from the iron that dominated his life. But nothing he had experienced during that time, none of the visions of wakefulness or the wonders of a dreamscape turned awry matched this vista.

A sound akin to laughter washed through his brain. Scowl stood up. He was naked apart from IronScythe and her smaller sister held tightly in his hands. A blob-like creature floated before him, a translucent gob of quivering flesh within which colours came and went. Many tentacles wriggled and squirmed, dancing in a rhythm that reminded him of the Carline's weirding, her gramarye. Power dwelled in its peculiar shape. The thing's control over this place was similar to that of a spider squatting upon the twitch-thread of its web. At its side hovered an old crone—Fulminara!

"You treat my choice with disdain?" said the ancient-looking Carline, her voice a dry croak.

Again laughter. *I sent you for a champion and you choose another such as yourself for this contest?* Gibbus flushed brown irritation and quivered as if in apoplexy. *Even I, Dimension Lord Gibbus, with my Hive behind me and my dimension mastery afore, have quailed at the monsters I have witnessed underneath the enormous panorama of my search—And you bring this?* The rotund body flung a dismissive tentacle in the direction of Scowl.

The rich red glows from the Morassic Seas turned Fulminara's features into crimson defiance. "In all my travels, across my own world and others, I have not yet found any monster or any power exceeding that of humankind. Vested in this champion I set before you are all the qualities humankind possesses in abundance."

Gibbus turned the livid grey of contemplation. *If your kind is so powerful, then why do you not fight upon your own behalf?*

"That is the beauty of my race; we are all things and nothing. We are love and hate, life and death, darkness and light. We are all made differently. Pain sits inside my champion, anger and retribution combined with a ruthlessness borne from his own desire for doom. At his side is a weapon crafted by humankind, and more powerful than the hand that wields it."

Scowl lifted up IronScythe. The She-blade remained unchanged in this weird landscape: solid, intractable, dangerous and unyielding. "Where, in all the darkness of delving, is this?"

Fulminara ignored him. "I stake my future existence upon this champion. Even if I lose, there will at least be pleasure in his performance. He is made for combat and dealing out death."

"Where am I?" Blackbeak repeated. "Answer me, witch!"

Fulminara turned towards him. "We are in the Plane of Realities—and to trip the planes is like to dream. You are here at my bidding, to do my bidding. You are my champion and how fine you look in your true form." A whisper from the Carline's lips and the air in front of

Scowl curved into a shimmering mirror. "See yourself as you truly are."

Scowl stared into the flickering glass. A handsome man with proud, defiant eyes, a noble nose and a wide, well-proportioned jaw glowered back at him. The face belonged to a king, not a dark, lonely slayer.

"Here, in the planes, you show your *Inner,*" explained Fulminara. "This is who you really are, Scowl. Whom you could have been if not so blighted by deformity and woe. And you and the scythe-blade are as real here as upon Arn itself."

"My Inner?"

"Your ethereal form, your essence. A wonder to behold."

Scowl thrust IronScythe into the gossamer-like mirror and it dissipated into the thick air as ribbons of silvery white. "Never show me this again."

Fulminara nodded, her eyes furrowing. "So be it."

Blackbeak pointed his poniard at the colour-god. "Who or what is this foul demon?"

Fulminara laughed. "This 'foul demon' is Dimension Lord Gibbus. He has dominion here. He trapped and entwined me, as I ensnared you. You are here as my champion to fight for my life."

"Why should I do such a thing?"

"Because I request you to."

"That is no argument. I have been brought here against my will."

"You are my champion. Accept your fate or never return."

"A threat?"

"A promise. 'Tis not I who threaten you, but Lord Gibbus and his champion. You must defeat his advocate to free us both."

Gibbus flushed with beige annoyance. *The creature that fights for me has no such pretensions; it is a thing of horrors that lusts for violence. It possesses no mind, only an over-powering desire for destruction. But I grow weary. The time for contest is here.*

Scowl's beady eyes focused upon the ancient Carline. "I shall be your champion, for I perceive no other alternative. But be warned, witch, after I win, IronScythe will sing for your blood."

CROWSFLIGHT

THOUSANDS OF angry crows surrounded Vareena. At first, she had marvelled at the birds swarming above. Now, running headlong across the empty, snow-covered plain towards a single outcrop of rock, she was certain her life was in danger.

Vareena had heard fanciful tales of babies stolen by eagles or hawks. Of small animals carried away by similar birds of prey. Crows loved to peck at those unfortunates hanging from Jhaz'Elrad's gibbet, and were often seen shadowing armies—a sign of doom in any land. For the birds to attack like this was unheard of.

She was a fast runner, eating up the ground with smooth efficiency. She hoped for a cave, a depression to defend, even a snowdrift to crawl into—anything other than this exposed plain.

A flurry of beating wings and incessant cries. The crows fell upon her. The weight of their concentrated numbers sent Vareena sprawling into the snow. She collapsed facedown, shielding her face from sharp black beaks. The sound of feathers and their incessant cawing was deafening. They dug their claws into the thick fur of her purloined over-uniform. Covering her back, arms and legs.

Thousands of wings beat in unison. Vareena risked a glance and saw only the black-green sheen of feathers. With a jolt, she was lifted skywards.

"No!" She flailed, trying to dislodge the crows. Higher she rose, as more winged bodies joined the effort. She was carried into the sky until—

She was at one with them.

An urgent, pushing necessity filled her mind. Cold air blew into her hair and face, but instead of a simple breeze, she recognised wind patterns and eddies, pressure changes and updrafts. She was aware of nothing but the thrill of flying and an intense sense of purpose.

"I'm coming," she whispered as a thousand crows carried her ever upward.

THE NEEDLE

GIBBUS' TENTACLES danced in mimicry of the Fulminara's gramarye. The air twisted and curled like heated glass.

An enormous slab of red and black flesh emerged through what Scowl now realised was a door to yet another dimension. It slammed into the ground, sending a booming pulse across the cloud ridden beach. Another slab—a whale-like foot of some kind— and a torso seemingly created from the whisperings of a lunatic's most disjointed hallucinations emerged. A pillar of gelatinous meat struggling to hold its form under the millstone of its own weight. The twin slabs were not legs, but two buttresses of thick bulging fat. The head was an extra mound of flesh sinking at its centre to create a corpulent hole.

A mouth or an eye?

Scowl took an involuntary step backwards and then another. The thing towered above him, four or five times his height. Two flaps of skin hung from either side of a bulbous neck. Almost as if they were wings. *Can this vile monster fly?*

'Wings, torso, head and feet' …convenient terms to describe the alien before him. The creature existed outside all logic and sense. Blackbeak raised IronScythe—a needle against a giant—and stood his ground. The monster remained impassive, inert. "Your champion does not want to fi—"

A vague, blurred shape enveloped Scowl. A cloying, living fog—some ghost-like apparition attached to the monster by an almost invisible tendril feeding it with the force of inflation. With a sweep of his blade Blackbeak severed the link. The half-formed blob fell at his feet.

Another appendage flew at him with considerable force, knocking him backwards. He rolled, landing in a defensive crouch. He twisted to the side and thrust the She-blade forwards with a vicious jerk of his arm, once again severing the connection.

An overpowering silence dominated the contest. The creature made no sound, it neither rasped nor moaned. Even the ripple of its constantly undulating flesh was muted. Scowl found the quietude disturbing. "Fight me face to face or not at all!" he shouted, pulling himself to full height.

In answer, his opponent rose upon its perverse, stridulating wings. It flew directly upwards, floated for a second and slammed down into the ground. The shockwave knocked Blackbeak over. A multitude of attacking gossamer tentacles radiated from his opponent's belly, quickly inflating with more red and black flesh. Smothering him. The attack was not one of cut, stab or thrust, but of suffocation.

"Is this how your champion fights!" Scowl yelled at Gibbus. He swung IronScythe and his poniard in twin deadly arcs, slicing through the outlandish flesh, cutting off vast gobs of fat. "It is a coward, like all those who face iron!" Where he slashed a connecting thread, more followed. He glanced at the beast, dismayed to see a vast tangle of threads erupting from its belly like an explosion.

Am I to be defeated by sheer force of numbers alone?

The tide of skin landed upon him in a choking cloud of ectoplasm. Ensnared, he gasped for breath. Gibbus' champion took to the air again, this time flying above him. Pulling Scowl towards the awful hole in the creature's face.

He struggled within the prison of living flesh, but he was trapped, beaten, lost…

Somewhere in the distance, he heard a dreadful laugh and Dimension Lord Gibbus' pouches slapped open and shut in a mimicry of applause.

THE REFLECTION

VAREENA LANDED atop a truncated stone spire in the centre of a vast crater. With loud squawks and calls, the crows released their grip and flew away. She fell to her knees, and came back to herself.

What on Arn just happened? Like waking from a vivid yet distant dream, she struggled to remember. A vague recollection of wind, of beating wings, of a freedom now lost, flitted across her mind. *The crows. They brought me here. Why?*

She knelt on the fringes of a silver-green forest. Dusk. She checked her backpack before the light disappeared. Everything was as it should be. Food. Tent. Her bag of priceless gems.

The little wood crested a flat-topped rock jutting from the midst of a black forest that crawled around its immense base. She located steps leading down, but had no desire to descend.

The trees faced inwards, circling a central copse where a solitary stone stood snarled by thick, twisted ivy and branches. Night was short and despite her recent experience, she needed sleep. She pitched the tent in the curious clearing and fell into deep slumber.

When she emerged, fully refreshed for the first time in weeks, the sun was past midday and the Coldstar lurking just below the horizon.

Snow had fallen in the night, covering the wood in a hoary shroud. She made a quick meal. Behind her, Eltirren crested the crater's rim, sending bright, horizontal rays through the forest, limning the lith-stone in white. Something glinted back, an arc-shaped reflection. She shielded her eyes against the blinding light, taking a step towards the ivy-encrusted centre-stone. Standing upon tiptoes, she pushed her head close to a mixture of branches and put a steadying hand against a dark timber. She screamed and jumped backwards. It was not wood that she touched, but wet material behind which something cold and fleshy lurked. She tore at the ivy, ripping aside the woody stems to reveal IronScythe. And around the blade's curved pommel? A frozen hand.

"No!" she howled, her voice swallowed by the covering of numbing snow. She cut away at the clogging greenery and twisted, entwining timbers with her fenneral sword and peered straight into the dead face of Scowl. His skin glistened like wet leather, melt-water dripping in a steady stream from his ice-caked hair. His iron-blue eyes were open, staring. *He can't be gone. He can't.* Vareena clasped her mouth in a convulsive movement and sunk to her knees. Another body lay at Scowl's feet—a beautiful naked woman. Tree roots twisted protectively around the snow-covered red-haired figure, who betrayed life from lips dancing with whispers.

Vareena picked up a stick and prodded the frozen girl. The body twitched and lips hissed. The stick was whipped from Vareena's startled fingers by some unseen force.

The weirding? Can it be possible.? The woman is a long-forgotten Carline? Then Scowl is not dead, he must be the prisoner of her wording!

Vareena's gaze fell upon Blackbeak's broken features. Even with half his face covered by black, snow-matted hair, he was a disgusting sight. *Why do I care for him? Does he need or want my help?* Her brows knitted together in resignation. *I'm here, brought by weirding or some other artistry of the Carline. I'll do whatever I can.*

She lifted her sword to slash again at the vines holding him. *I'll free him and take him far away from this place.*

Behind her, the Carline whispered malevolently. A tree root came to life, looping around Vareena's blade. Another root lurched from the mud, encircling the hilt, wrenching it from her fingers and dragging the sword into the tangled undergrowth. Angry and undaunted, she threw herself at the jumble of branches that held Scowl. The limbs were solid and unyielding.

Vareena sat down and shivered. She thought of freeing IronScythe, of using the She-blade against the Carline, yet some preternatural force protected the two from any attack or help she could give.

Night came and went and still she sat. After a full day of silent watching and growing helplessness, she returned to her tent and spent the next few hours in fitful sleep.

Another day passed. Then another. She never stirred from Scowl's side except to sleep or make her toilet. When she slept, it was in fits and bursts. Sometimes she would wake choking, fearing the trees had also made her their prisoner, wondering what had happened to bring her to this cold, inert place. A week passed and her resolve gradually disappeared, consumed by terrible inaction. Her food supplies were almost exhausted. *I must leave–and soon.* Her inability to help, cut deep. *Why bring me here if I can do nothing?* She threw herself upon Scowl and sobbed at her uselessness.

A tear fell from her green eyes and splashed on Scowl's cold, outstretched half-hand. She hugged him, wanting to give her outlandish friend some of her own warmth. Her hand reached out to the outstretched pommel of IronScythe, encircling his. She stared into his impassive ugly face and kissed him.

Ironlight

BLACKBEAK CHOKED, suffocating under the assault of flesh spewing from the belly of Gibbus' champion. The thing lay on top of him. Crushing.

I am done. Finished.

And then a glow surrounded him, illuminating the creature's underbelly with searing white.

The IronLight?

It was something invested in iron itself. Many times in the midst of battle, its sheen had licked unbidden along his blade. But never had its appearance brought such strength and power. And where the light touched? The creature's flesh boiled. The She-blade cut with a preternatural force. He hacked and sliced at swathe upon swathe of blubber, fought until he fell free, coughing and spluttering onto the weird beach. He took a deep breath, and pulled himself to shaky feet.

The monster lay before him, struggling to fly, wings flapping. Blackbeak flung his poniard aside and charged, the blinding glare of the IronLight burning from the She-blade like a bright, terrible star. He brought the blade down in a two-handed attack, cleaving the wings into useless flaps of riven flesh.

Gibbus' champion writhed, its creeping protoplasm trying to escape in ballooning tendrils. Scowl's bright blade showed no mercy. IronScythe swung repeatedly, slicing with a casual grace that dismembered as easily as if she were quartering a hide. Soon, all that was left of the monster was a quivering pile of dismembered blubber.

Blackbeak, his chest heaving, retrieved his poniard and approached Fulminara and the colour-god. He said nothing, although his iron-blue eyes stared at the Carline with undisguised malice.

Fulminara wore a shocked expression, eyeing her champion and his still shining blade with pride. "The contest is decided."

Gibbus' skin swirled with dark purple hues.

"My champion is the victor," Fulminara continued. "You will not interfere with my dimension or myself again. As was our agreement."

Purple washed to deep red. The colour-god quivered. *No.*

"You go back upon your word?"

You forget. I am the master of many and you are the master of only one.

"I will not let you keep me. I'm no-one's slave."

Let me congratulate you, your champion was most impressive. This Scowl shall serve me well.

"We had an agreement."

In your dimension, such notions of honour are no doubt important. I possess no similar weakness—another sign of my natural dominance. You will join my Hive and submit to my superior will.

"Never!"

Gibbus flushed deepest black. A multitude of creatures materialized, hanging faintly in the air, encircling the colour-god.

See how my Hive comes at my command? With your spirit in my collection, I'll have dominance in your world and will trip it when I please. Have I told you how I feed? How I seek out the mind's essence and suck it into my being? I devour every tender morsel of thought and taste every emotion. I will feast on you, Fulminara and—

IronScythe stabbed the Dimension Lord. Scowl twisted her with relish. Colours leaked out of Gibbus, spilling onto the beach. The IronLight burned them away, cauterizing every one of the creature's hues and stealing its rainbow. The thirty-six stalked eyes strained as if trying to escape, then fell limp. The colour-god shrivelled into a dried out husk.

Gibbus' Hive squealed and groaned, a peculiar threnody of squeaks, moans and rattles. The spirits, taken from countless dimensions—the prisoners of the Dimension Lord—faded, returning to the realities they were stolen from.

Blackbeak raised the She-blade and advanced upon Fulminara.

"No Scowl, you cannot attack me. Without the help of the Carline, you will never return home. Besides, I am now in your debt and will aid you in kind."

IronScythe lowered and the light fell from the blade.

An expression of relief crossed the old crone's face. "Yours is a strange unseen soul. Its shadows haunt and worry. You hide amongst them. Where can such resolve, such power, come from?"

Scowl looked at his blade and shrugged. "Let us leave this place."

"You have not answered."

"Iron is its own reward if handled justly and with honour and pride."

WHEN AND WHERE

Scowl returned to the sound of sobbing mixing in and out of the Carline's gramarye. Cold engulfed him. He shivered violently.

"You're back!"

"I'm blind," Scowl croaked from a dry, barren throat. As he spoke, the blackness disappeared and he was rewarded by the vision of Vareena. She was red-eyed and tear-stained. Her thick lips parted in a relieved, yet pained smile.

He blinked. "Vareena?"

"Yes!"

"How—?"

"I found you."

His memory returned. "Where are you, Fulminara!" he shouted, struggling against his bonds, the lifeless eyes now sparkling with fury.

Vareena stepped back, whirling around to find the naked Carline now free of the forest's embrace. She held Vareena's white sword, her hand encircling the fenneral blade without threat.

"Who are you?" said Fulminara, stepping closer to Vareena.

"She is nothing to do with you, witch," croaked Scowl.

One, long-nailed hand pushed Vareena's lank hair back from her face. "Ah—now I realise. I chose well for my champion—little did I realise he'd call upon such a powerful ally."

"W-what—?" stammered Vareena.

"Yes, my lovely—*you*."

"I don't understand."

"You wouldn't, it is far too early for you to *Show!*" The Carline threw back her head and laughed into the forest. As if in answer, the trees rustled, whilst crows cawed in the sky above.

"No!" cried Scowl. "You are mistaken."

The witch's head dropped and turned towards the lith-stone and her prisoner. "Do you not feel the girl's fledgling majiks? Or are you blinded by your iron? Your blade will always attract such *baggage*."

The woman's words were dreamy, containing a trailing whisper that seemed at home in this glade.

"Who are you?" Vareena asked, staring into eyes of the same emerald green as her own.

"You already suspect the answer."

"The Carline are well-remembered in this land." Vareena's noble tones returned as she repeated the lesson learned as a child. "They were midwives and healers. They died out gyres past after they lost the war against Chicanery."

"Yes, we Carline once served the common good. Until Cairn made us their enemy—a war we could never win. Only those sanctioned by the Usery were allowed to practice the majiks—or so they told us. We were not as ruthless, nor as powerful as such concentrated

Chicanery, so we simply disappeared." Fulminara placed a delicate hand upon Vareena's shoulder. "Tell me, Mistress Vareena of Keep Krall, have you heard mention of *the gift of the Carline?*"

Vareena shook her head.

"No, Vareena." Scowl, struggled against the thick branches and ensnaring vines that still held him.

"We Carline possess a singular talent. Not even Chicanery, with its much vaunted majiks, can offer what we can. We divine the future."

"Do not listen," implored Scowl.

"We can predict two things," Fulminara continued, her hand cupping Vareena's cheek. "We foretell the *When* and *Where* of your death. I offer you this information without cost—all you need do is ask."

"This is how the witch plays with us," said Scowl. "You must resist."

The Carline smiled. "Consider it a reward for helping my champion."

Vareena pushed Fulminara's hand away. "I didn't do anything."

"Do you really believe that? Tell me—how did you come to be here? This is the fortress of the Carline. Impenetrable to all."

"You brought me here—didn't you?"

The witch's answer was to shake her head. "I am as surprised by your presence as is your dark friend."

"If you didn't bring me, then who did?"

Fulminara shrugged. "I would look no further than yourself."

"I don't understand."

"You are more powerful than you imagine, Mistress Krall, and yet the mystery of your appearance can be solved by accepting my gift. Do you want it or not?"

Scowl drew breath to speak, but, with a whisper from the Carline's lips, the vine encircling his throat tightened, silencing any protest he might have made.

Vareena nodded. Her heart quickening. "Tell me then, when and where, and be done with it."

Fulminara bowed. "You are a rarity, Vareena. The Gyre will pass untold times before one such as you will appear again. Your life shall be a stretched one, my pretty. You shall live many times the mortal span. One day you shall become She-savant and grace the hallowed halls of Chicanery at Cairn."

"What?"

"Oh my darling, you're so young, so fresh and innocent, but I can glimpse your end as clearly as I stare at you now." In a disembodied and powerful voice, as if speaking with the certainty of the grave, Fulminara said: "The Gyre shall pass forty-three times before you find death deep in the watery caves of the inland Lissem Sea."

Blackbeak gasped.

"She-Chicane?" murmured Vareena from the midst of a daze.

"Yes, girl. You must one day Show and join the Usery. Of what will befall you from hence onwards, I do not know—we Carline are gifted only with *When* and *Where*. Yours is a rare life. My champion has powerful friends indeed. My wait was not in vain."

Vareena fell to the forest floor and hugged her knees. "Forty-three passes of the Gyre? Impossible…"

"Not so Vareena, Chicanery are long-lived—and you shall become an elder amongst them." Fulminara turned to her trapped companion. "As for you, Scowl, I shall not make the same request. I know of who you are, yet I can perceive nothing in your future, nor nothing in your past. You do not belong to this world, that much is for sure."

"Then release me."

"Ah, if only I could. What fun we would enjoy, you and I. But I do not trust your iron. You hold a strange mixture of powers. Forgive me, but I will make my exit while I still can." She paused and gave him one last look. "We will meet again, Scowl. Be sure of it. And do not worry; the way out of my wooded fortress is open." She turned to Vareena, and held out the fenneral sword. "This is a fabled weapon, Vareena. It has a past and a future all of its own. It is of the earth and I hear it speak. You will call him 'Cowlsbane' and he will forever sit at your side. Many songs will be written about the She-Chicane and her gleaming sword of purest white."

Vareena took the proffered weapon, staring at the blade with stunned eyes. "Thank you."

Fulminara backed out of the glade and disappeared into shadowy tendrils of the forest.

A short while later, the witch's chanting gramarye whispered through the trees. Scowl collapsed to the ground, free from his living bonds.

Vareena pulled him to her tent. She made them a meal with the last of her food, while Blackbeak's clothing steamed in the heat of the fire. Fulminara's words hung heavily upon Vareena. *Can they be true?* She understood little of majiks, of Usery; other than they were connected closely to the land and extended life and learning. Yet there had been no doubt in the Carline. *Am I excited? Scared? Relieved?* And what about Keep Krall? Her revenge against Jhaz'Elrad seemed almost petty now. Irrelevant.

An hour passed as the two contemplated their various thoughts. Vareena's head shaking with disbelief,

Scowl rubbing his stiff limbs.

"The Coldstar rises later than I remember," said Blackbeak, breaking the silence.

"Later? Eight months have passed since you left Keep Krall. Eltirren has moved far in that time. Goldering has ended. We are now in Bluster, although her blizzards are late to come."

"Eight months? It is only weeks since I left your island citadel." He shook his head. "The weirding is indeed an eldritch force."

Vareena nodded, sensing a question upon Blackbeak's lips. "You want to ask me something?"

"What brought you here?"

"A long story. Being Keep Mistress was not as easy as I'd hoped—I was overthrown. I sought to follow you to Palimara, to employ mercenaries to win back what is rightfully mine, but became lost upon *The Salted Wastes.*" She remembered the crows and the flight to the Carline's stunted spire. "Something drew me here," she said, unwilling to tell him more.

"Your majiks," he said flatly.

To Vareena, it sounded like a rebuke. "Why do you hate Chicanery?"

"Look what they did to Fulminara. The Carline were peaceful until Chicanery intervened. I have seen too much of what the majiks have done to Arn. The devastation. The darkness."

"Then you'll grow to hate me too, won't you? If and when I reach my destiny."

He didn't answer.

"What happened between you and Fulminara?"

Scowl shrugged. "I was about to die. Beaten. Some force helped me in that moment and saved me. That was you, Vareena."

"I didn't do anything."

"Whatever you did, consciously or not—I am thankful." The words left Blackbeak's tongue with difficulty.

"So, the majiks have their use after all."

Scowl shrugged and changed the subject. "I do not trust Fulminara. We must leave this place as soon as possible."

"Yes, I'll accompany you to Palimara."

"We cannot travel together, Vareena."

"Why not?"

"Bad things happen around iron. It is folly for anyone to accompany me."

"Perhaps it's my destiny to continue upon this road, however much my presence annoys you."

The beak-face showed no feeling, no emotion. "Destiny will find you whatever direction you take. You must prepare yourself for what is to come. Not many know that one day they will Show."

Show—that word again. "What does it mean?"

"A rite of passage. The moment when a new savant unconsciously announces his majiks to the world, to Chicanery, who can hear the call over the length and breadth of Arn. He is sought out and taken to Cairn where his learning begins."

"*His majiks,* you say? I'm a woman—or haven't you noticed?"

"She-savants are few and far between, Vareena, and their history chequered."

"What does that mean?"

"You will find out."

"Then tell me of the Carline? How are they different?"

Scowl shrugged. "The majiks are many-sided," he

answered. "Not even I fully understand them."

"At last, something you don't know about."

"All the answers you need are to be found in Cairn, in the city of majiks. I suggest you make your way there as soon as we leave this place."

An agitated silence fell between them, finally broken by Vareena's angry, sharp words. "I'm not going to Cairn," she announced. "You owe me, Scowl. You will accompany me to Palimara and help me raise an army, for I will not let Jhaz'Elrad and his traitors take what belongs to me."

"Iron does not follow the whim of girls," he answered.

"Forget your damn iron for a moment and listen—I saved your life and that has to mean something to you. It has to."

Blackbeak's jaws clamped together in resignation. "You can travel with me to Palim," he said after a pause. "What you do once you are there is your own concern."

Vareena nodded, relieved. "Thank you, my friend."

Scowl replaced the hood upon his head. "Now let us make haste."

Together they left the Carline's glade and began the long trek to Palim.

The Scowl

THE SCOWL: PART THREE

GOD
GOLD

And they were taken to the Isle of Asbit, to his dark red, twisted tower whereupon evil was put unto them. They grew in size and mind, came to know what they were, and to feel unimaginable pain and suffering. But they escaped, thrived through terrible adversity, and the Margolyn became their home... And it was in this forest where they met the harna...

The Yarn of Gard, Cairn.

KRETCH!

"**NOW YOU** are what I call a nice bit o' weavery!" Vareena pushed back her long lank, blonde hair and eyed the obnoxious drunk with defiance. He had been causing trouble since she and her hooded companion had entered this shantytown tavern. It was a rough place, but Scowl's cold iron—a metal that put dread into all—and his ever-present hood, meant such squalid accommodation was the norm. They had not yet seen the room. It promised to be as dingy and unkempt as this over-filled bar.

"A toast! A toast to—?" The drunk stared at Vareena expectantly.

She turned away from the greasy-blonde ruffian whose face was red and stained, his fighting weave muddied. One hand rested on his thigh, the other proffered a dripping mug.

"A toast to the loveliest bit o' skin that has graced this bar in a long time." He drank from a wooden tankard before lurching towards them and sitting down. His breath stank of stale ale.

Vareena scowled, her lip curling in revulsion. Her features spoke of refinement and nobility, a natural beauty whose gruff-looking fighting-weaves gave an almost boyish allure. Many other eyes had caressed her lithe figure, but only Raza was fool enough to ignore her worrisome companion.

"Now darlin', give Raza a chance!" He laughed, a lecherous grin twisting his features. His attention turned to Scowl and the blank, iron-blue eyes staring through two ragged slits in his hood. "What 'ave we here?" he asked, sitting back. "Hey lads, I think this one's shy."

There were few laughs as most found the shrouded figure worrisome.

Raza turned his attention back to Vareena. "So, what's your story? Let me guess—a rich man's piece down on her luck, or some courtesan looking for some rough?"

Vareena sat back and smiled. Scowl had seen the expression before. He shook his head in warning.

"Cos if it's a bit of rough you're after, I'm your man." Raza licked at a well-worn hole in his top lip, his tongue missing whatever jewellery usually decorated the space.

"Go and find some urine-smelling pigsty to rot in, you drunken idiot, or you'll feel the flat of my blade."

"What?"

The slap came without warning and resounded loudly. "I said, get lost."

The dark tavern exploded in laughter.

Raza appeared nonplussed; the slap only seemed

to encourage him. His eyes narrowed. "Thinks you are better than us, do you? Well maybe you are, and maybe you're not. But maybe this will make you think otherwise." He produced a small lump of yellow metal from his stained weavery. It caught the dim cresset-light, gilding his features in amber.

Gold.

She was intrigued, suspicious. Gold was a forbidden substance; and these were miners.

"Not so haughty now, are you?"

Vareena shook her head, trying to rid herself of a sudden dizziness.

"Put that away, Raza," grumbled the Innkeeper, an overweight, baby-faced man whose bald pate shone with a thin pall of sweat. He wore a stained apron and little else. "You know what Jessop will do to you if he finds out."

Raza continued, undaunted. "I eat girls like her for breakfast, know what I mean?" He made an obscene gesture with his tongue.

Vareena grabbed the fleshy protuberance with swift fingers, twisting viciously. The drunk's eyes popped, but he still smiled. "You'll learn some manners when talking to your betters," she said in clear, noble tones. She pushed him backwards. He fell with a clatter, breaking the wooden chair.

Scowl closed his eyes and groaned.

Raza rubbed his tongue with relish. "I like a lass who puts up a fight." In one quick movement, he was back upon shaky feet, an inelegant but well-kept stone sword held threateningly in his outstretched hand. "You'll pay for that, my young lady—with a kiss!"

"Raza! For the sake of the Gyre, let the girl be!" shouted the Innkeeper.

"I can look after myself." Vareena pushed their table over and sprang into a fighter's crouch. Beer and their uneaten meal crashed onto the floor.

Scowl cursed under his breath, covering his long curved blade of iron with his cape.

Vareena brandished Scowlsbane, her well-carved and balanced sword of magnificent white. Such unblemished stone was rare indeed and worth a king's ransom, but the value was not just aesthetic. Crystal purity gave strength to the blade, preventing it from shattering during battle. Black-fenneral was its master, but the best sword was only equal to the flesh wielding it. Vareena was a trained fighter.

Bowing to the encircled crowd, Raza made a flourish with his arm. Vareena's booted foot sent him flying. He hit the floor hard and lay there for a few moments. When he got up, all trace of humour had gone. Someone put a friendly hand on his shoulder. "Leave it man, come 'ere and share a drink." He shrugged it off, eyes ablaze with anger. Blood leaked from a cut lip.

"Raza!" warned the Innkeeper.

Vareena measured her opponent. *Drunk yes, but lithe with a balanced physique. His sword is well oiled. As is he. I'll have some fun teaching him manners.*

The drunk crashed in upon Vareena, not expecting the sudden shift of weight that took her beyond his thrust and gave room and time for her to slap him across his backside with the flat of her blade.

Unable to resist this second opportunity, she kicked him to the floor again. He jumped up with a spring, flying at her. Vareena dodged, tripping over the upturned table. She regained her balance just in time to parry a vicious slice to her throat.

Raza battered murderously upon her sword. Hot

sparks from both blades bathed the drunk's enraged features in a dancing array of flashing shards. They revealed something evil in the man, some debased thing inhabiting his leering, creased face.

Vareena crumpled under this fenneral hammering, parrying with defensive grace. Raza sweated heavily, his breath laboured. The barrage faltered, Vareena slipped under his blade and punched him in the face with her hilted fist. He went down, yelping like a dog, his sweaty hands clutching at a broken nose. His sword fell with a clatter.

"That'll teach you to watch your words in future, if nothing else. Now get out." She kicked his blade to the door, and returned to the table.

A few moments later, the ruffian was thrown into the street. Raza lingered outside for a while, moaning and shouting with equal vehemence, before disappearing into the late night of cold winds smattered with snow.

Vareena righted their table and sat down with her sable-weaved companion. She patted her sword, staring at him with pride and expectancy. As usual, his features were hidden—she could not fathom his thoughts.

"Next time flirt, and save yourself the trouble." His voice was cold and emotionless.

"Flirt with every smelly drunk just so you can eat in peace? I'd rather die."

"If you go on in your present manner, you probably will. I was nearly forced to intervene; and iron is the nemesis of delving, not drunks. I had wanted to talk to the man. There was something about him."

"It's not my fault we've to stay in this dive. I've enough wealth to afford better lodgings. It's you they don't like."

A few men looked up.

"Keep your highborn voice down. Soon, we will be in Palim. You can then find more luxurious rooms."

Vareena dreaded reaching Palimara's capital. They were to part there, or so he had said many weeks ago, before their long passing of *The Grikes*—a vast, broken land of exposed, cracked rock. "I'm sorry." Her hand reached out to his masked face but, as ever, he pulled away. She stared at their spilled food. "Oh."

"Yes, I'm afraid our dinner is on the floor. Perhaps your great wealth can pay for a replacement, Mistress Vareena of Keep Krall."

She was about to tell him otherwise, when a shiver shot down her spine.

Scowl's head twitched towards the wooden entranceway, his keen but misshapen nose sniffing the air.

A gust of wind, and the door opened to a hairy monstrosity. An animal was framed there, a deformed creature whose large eyes took in the tavern scene with one great sweep of its bull-head.

"Kretch!" Vareena gasped, her hand again moving to the sure white fenneral at her side.

Ill-wrought ears pricked and pointed in her direction, while eyes, fringed by abundant fur sought her out.

A demon straight from childhood fairy tales, a bugbear akin to the bogeyman that haunted deep night, darkly lit rooms and forbidden holes, stared right at her. The Kretch were monsters from myth, used to frighten children into obedience. But here was the monster made real. She drew breath to shout, but Scowl covered her mouth with his gloved half-hand and shook his head.

Vareena was terrified, but the men in the tavern showed only resentment. *They are used to this creature's presence*. She guessed they would not tolerate it for long.

The Innkeeper remained unmoved, his expression grim.

The thing lurched forward, uneven legs twisting in unnatural but well-practised rhythm. Muscles bulged and knotted awkwardly. One leg had too many joints. The other was thicker, nothing more than fur-wrapped bone covered in a dense network of arteries and tangled lines of rope-like sinew. It shuddered and shook as it lumbered closer. The movement sickened Vareena. It was impossible to make sense of the dark-grey, furry limbs.

The tavern became hushed as the creature approached the bar. Long muscled arms brushed against chairs and tables. It wore a weave of some kind, beaded with red, azure, orange and grey. Vareena gasped, for at its side hung an enormous wedge of roughly hewn fenneral. She possessed a passion for weaponry of all kinds and this was a magnificent specimen. A mixture of pure white and black banded stone. The true beauty had not been realised by the carver and, intentional or not, its roughness served as a sharp reminder of its function.

"What on Arn is it?" Vareena whispered through Scowl's stunted fingers.

"He is a kerrish."

The name meant nothing to her.

The creature spoke, its voice low and un-Arnish in cadence, reverberating from within its enormous barrel-like chest like a growl. "Innkeeper, Ya'ousa search for one called Raza. To him, Ya'ousa must speak. You seen Raza?"

"I've told you, we don't want your sort in here. Get out before I kick you out myself!"

"Ya'ousa must find Raza." The kerrish glanced around at all the upturned faces. "He miner. Ya'ousa just want speak." A short, stubby snout opened to reveal a set of white, canine teeth and blackened gums.

Vareena shuddered.

The Innkeeper's eyes flicked at Vareena and Scowl with silent warning. "I have never seen nor heard of this Raza."

"You speak untruth." The animal sniffed, his black nose crinkling. "Ya'ousa smell lies in your breath and sweat. Tell Ya'ousa where Raza is, and Ya'ousa will not return."

The bulging head brushed the ceiling with fur. A powerful creature, yet Vareena sensed vulnerability. As if the stares of so many hate-filled eyes somehow weakened it.

The fat-bellied innkeeper shook his head. He reached down under the bar and produced an evil-looking wooden club. A rustle behind the kerrish, and the other men readied their weapons.

A change came over the creature then, a calmness. Scowl cursed before getting up and pulling Vareena behind him.

"Ya'ousa thirsty. Long way back to his camp. You give Ya'ousa water."

The innkeeper patted the club into the palm of his hand. "We don't serve the likes of you in here. Now go while you still have the legs to carry you."

"A drink of water and Ya'ousa will leave in peace, yes?"

The Innkeeper's expression turned to one of grim violence, but before he could act, a nasal voice spoke from the shadows. "A mug of water for my friend." Scowl moved out of the smoke-filled murk and stood next to the peculiar creature.

Animalistic eyes searched the hooded features with a mixture of unease and wonder.

"Are you deaf? A mug of water," Scowl repeated.

"I don't serve his kind. He aint natural. You'd best to keep out of this if you know what's good for you."

"And what is good for me?"

The Innkeeper swung his club, but Scowl caught the wood in his perverse-looking half-hand and wrenched it from the astonished fat man's fingers. He nodded to the kerrish and, grabbing Vareena, they made a rush for the door. A few men tried to stop them. The lump-like paws of Ya'ousa knocked them aside as if they were children. Scowl whirled the wooden club around him like a living thing.

They burst into the street with an angry mob in pursuit. "What are you doing?" shrieked Vareena. "Why are you helping this creature?"

Scowl ignored her.

Raza appeared, his face full of anger, a group of ten men standing at his back.

"So, you're in cahoots with this inquisitive Kretch? I should've guessed. Come on lads, let's finish this here!"

Something in his manner angered Vareena. Before, Raza had been a loud and harmless drunk, now, with others to support him, an evil streak showed itself. Vareena took a deep breath and threw herself straight at him, slashing and hacking at his blade. He stumbled backwards in shock, parrying. A whirl of flashing blades in which Raza was but a minor player. A shiny object dropped from his hand, distracting him. Vareena plunged her sword deep into his rib cage, crunching bones and twisting viciously. Blood spurted, bathing her in crimson. Raza gurgled for a moment, and crumpled to the ground. Reaching down, she grabbed at the object that had been the cause of his downfall and hid it in her weaves. She pulled the fenneral free and stared into Raza's lifeless face. The horror of what she had done hit like a thrown rock upon the back of her head.

The mob howled in derision at the sight of the dead miner and charged towards them.

"You little fool!" Scowl shouted, snatching her sword from her limp fingers and throwing the club away. "We might have been able to disappear into the night, but now these men will want revenge."

Ya'ousa unleashed his bludgeon of fenneral. "Follow!" he barked with command. The kerrish broke through the massed men, and rushed down an enclosed alley. Scowl doubted this strategy but had no time to consider its merit. They reached the back wall of a squat, wooden building. Ya'ousa flung himself onto the roof.

His legs are not as weak as they seem, thought Vareena.

Ya'ousa lowered a muscled arm and scooped her up before she had time to protest. Blackbeak needed no such assistance and ascended to the roof with ease.

They ran across the rooftops, disturbing more inhabitants below. The mob grew in size and volume, filling the narrow streets with howls and shouting. Ya'ousa remained unperturbed. In one deft movement, he bounded down into a bramble thicket and revealed a hollow, a hiding place.

The horde rushed past.

A few minutes later they were on their way again. This time the kerrish lead them upwards, away from the shantytown of Fisk and its angry inhabitants.

Fire

"YOU EAT." The kerrish thrust a rough wooden bowl at Vareena.

She examined the contents with worry.

"It good."

The creature had strung only a few words together since their escape, but they had willingly followed him to his camp hidden in a small glade on the hillside. It looked down on the red-orange fires and thick smokes of the small shantytown they had so recently departed, a long brown stain upon the thin covering of snow. Fisk sat to the north-west of Palim.

Ya'ousa's tent, constructed from skins and tanned pelts held together by a tight latticework of thongs, was foreign to Vareena. Roughly painted marks adorned its surface, enormous paw prints of blue, red, orange and yellow on the white, black and tan of the furs. A haven of warmth. She allowed herself to relax.

Ya'ousa came back with another bowl, and stared at the cross-legged hooded man whose sable weavery somehow fitted these outlandish surroundings. "Ya'ousa not mention before but why your face covered?"

"He prefers it that way," said Vareena.

The kerrish ignored her. "Is insult to Ya'ousa, insult to his tent, to his food."

"Forgive me, Ya'ousa. I wear my hood against the hatred of other men."

"Hatred? Yes, Ya'ousa know of what you speak. He sees it across the lands of man. Aversion, loathing—all these things. Yet kerrish too are not free of this evil. Ya'ousa say, remove hood. Let him see who you are, let him judge."

Scowl placed his hand on the hilt of IronScythe, and caressed the delving metal.

Vareena sensed the meaning: only iron had ever been his friend. She was young, an annoying hindrance to him, but she understood his pain.

Blackbeak nodded and in one deft movement, the hood was gone.

A single stranding burned in the hide-encased darkness, flickering in gentle homage to the wind gusting outside. Warm orange light bathed Scowl's naked face in velvety hues and delicate shadow. Even this lambent glow could not diminish the abomination revealed lurking there.

Ya'ousa studied the smashed, misshapen features— the blackened beak-nose, the crooked eyes and leering mouth—with curiosity.

Vareena, intimate with Scowl's looks, still shuddered involuntarily. Such heinous, viscerally repellent features would always shock. *But I have grown to care for them.*

"Yes, Ya'ousa thinks he understands. Men do not like difference. They want everything to be same. Is why they do not take to kerrish. Too much deformity in us bred from our beginnings many, many passes ago. But from adversity comes humility. From hardship, comes strength and resolve. Yes?"

Scowl cast a wry eye in the direction of the furred face. Ya'ousa's long, white whiskers twitched proudly against black and grey striped fur. He nodded.

With her perfect limbs and fine features, Vareena felt guilty listening to these words. She had tried to understand Scowl, to understand what effect appearing as an atrocity to other men and women might have upon her own sensibilities. But it was impossible. She was his antithesis, his opposite, and that was as close as she could ever get.

"I am different," Blackbeak croaked, his face blushing in uneven red over the thick welts of his scarred flesh. Under his cowl, he was confident, powerful. Exposed like this, his embarrassment made Vareena's heart melt.

Taking the stranding in reverent paws, the kerrish lit a small bowl of incense. "We eat now." The collection of dried leaves, seeds and berries fizzed and spluttered, filling the air with vapours not conducive to eating.

Vareena coughed and her eyes watered.

Ya'ousa paid her no concern. He joined them, bending his legs awkwardly.

She studied her food again. She dipped in a wooden spoon and took a wary sniff of the contents.

Scowl caught her expression. "My companion's trust is not so easily given. She is a curious sort, and eager to find out who you are, my friend."

"I didn't say that," Vareena protested, forcing a spoonful into her mouth.

"But question is on your mind, yes?"

Vareena nodded, not bothering to hide a grimace at the taste of the grim broth.

"Where Ya'ousa comes from, fighting together

proves friendship. After battle, we share food as sign of trust. Only then are formal introductions made. But Ya'ousa bow to man's way." He put his bowl down and placed enormous paws on his chest. "This is Jantiff Ya'ousa of Totu Cland. Powerful Cland. Ya'ousa is kerrish from Northern land of Skourass, wherein sits beautiful forest of Margolyn." He spread his arms around him in a magnificent arc. "Big forest. Mother to all Ya'ousa's race. Home. But you, man-girl, you called Ya'ousa by other name."

"Kretch?"

Scowl glared at Vareena. "Forgive her, Ya'ousa, she does not know what that word means."

"Yes I do," she answered, spitting out bits of food. "The Kretch are animals who come from holes of delving. As a child, Melaina, my nanny, told me they came at night to eat naughty children."

"Ya'ousa is no Kretch! Has never been. They were an evil from long time ago. No more Kretch, they gone. You understand?" Ya'ousa's breath rasped in the smoky gloom. "Yes?"

"You give Ya'ousa the worst insult, Vareena," said Scowl.

Vareena sat back, a worried expression on her face. "I'm sorry, but how was I supposed to know? I'm not like you, Scowl, who has knowledge of everything, every place and everyone. You are no older than me. When did you find the time to become so informed?"

Blackbeak shrugged. "All I know I learned upon the Bacchust Isle."

The kerrish made a gruff sound in his throat. "Ya'ousa never heard of such place."

"It's a myth, a fancy of old befuddled sailors," interjected Vareena. "The island doesn't exist."

"I awoke there." Scowl stared up into the shadowy recesses of the tent. "Although my memories are sparse."

"Then you, too, must have been befuddled," Vareena mocked. "'The beautiful but lost Bacchust Isle' is a familiar theme of those who make a feeble living begging down by the docks in Fangarra. A fable from the dreams of the deranged."

Blackbeak dismissed her comments with a shake of his head. "You wanted an introduction, Ya'ousa. Then let me give it. I have many names, but most know me as Scowl."

Ya'ousa bowed. "And what of the man-girl?" he asked, impatient with the exchange. "Who you?"

"I am Mistress Vareena Krall of Oldiva," she replied in her finest noble tones.

"Good," the kerrish boomed. "We share food and introductions. We now friends."

Silence descended while they ate. In the quiet of the meal, the dying face of Raza came repeatedly to Vareena's mind. An odious part of her psyche had revelled in the death. Blood still stained her weaves. Its salty smell pulsed within her nostrils, even under the burning incense. *I killed before, when escaping Keep Krall. A necessity, but I wanted to kill Raza.* A thrill shuddered through her, akin to those first few nights with Steward Allon, her only lover. But this was lust of a different kind. She had not been herself since entering the seedy tavern. She was tense, fevered and her heart thudded over-loud in her chest.

After they had finished, Ya'ousa took their bowls and scrubbed at them in some dark corner. He returned and crouched upon a cured hide. Vareena tried to read his features, but could glean nothing from his animalistic expression.

"Tell me Ya'ousa," said Scowl. "What was your interest in this man, Raza?"

The kerrish cocked his head to one side as if debating the merits of this question. "Ya'ousa must find him. Is all."

"I killed him," said Vareena, ashamed by the hint of pride coating her words. "The man was a letch and a fool."

"Raza was the dead man?" Ya'ousa shook his bullhead and the light left his eyes. "Then all Ya'ousa has done now turned to dust." His claws pulled into two, enormous fists and Vareena feared he would hit out at her.

"Why were you searching for him?" asked Scowl. "And in such a dangerous tavern?"

"Enough. Before Ya'ousa answer, he too has question: Why you help Ya'ousa, why you put yourself in danger for kerrish, eh?"

"The answer is a single word—gold."

Ya'ousa scowled, his paw reaching for the smooth haft of his fenneral club. "Then you are like him, like all men. Ya'ousa tried to ignore what is against your thigh. Delving metals are not hidden easily. Leave now. Go, or Raza shall not be only casualty this night!" He bounded up, his club swinging in one commanding claw.

Scowl did not react.

Why is he not afraid of this monster? thought Vareena, grasping her blade.

"Sit down, Ya'ousa," Blackbeak commanded. The club hung only a sword width from his ruined nose. "Yes, I am interested in gold, but my interest is in returning it back to the earth, where such evil belongs."

"Why should Ya'ousa believe? You like other men hungry for delving metals."

"Raza was a troublemaker and a drunk. Yet before Vareena sent him on his way, he showed her a lump of the forbidden metal. The miners tried to hush him up, and I have a nose for such things."

Vareena fingered her weaves guiltily. The gold weighed in her pocket. Knowing it was there thrilled her.

"Another name was mentioned: *Jessop.*"

"Jessop! Yes, Ya'ousa has heard speak of this man."

Scowl motioned for Ya'ousa to sit. "We fought together, shared food and honour. Our trust is proven. Your own laws bind you as I am bound to my bane of iron. Put your club away, Ya'ousa my friend, and tell me your story. I may find a way to help."

The mound of foreboding muscle and fur, pondered these words. "Trust is never easy for kerrish, despite pretty speak. But Ya'ousa put away his fenneral."

"You will trust me. I swear upon my iron that my words are true."

"What is the worth of trust when all hope is gone?"

Vareena couldn't control her curiosity any longer. "Why were you looking for Raza? The man was an idiot, a drunken fool."

The kerrish turned sorrowful eyes towards her. "Ya'ousa search for his Clandsriders, his brethren. They are slaves in some mine of fenneral near here, in broken region known as *The Grikes*. Evil men make them work in deep dark holes. Many mines in this land. Ya'ousa not know where to look. And no one will help a Kretch." He paused, his face showing pain even underneath its thick covering of grey fur.

"Continue," whispered Scowl. "We are your friends."

"Ya'ousa employ thief who visited town where mining men go. Fisk. He found nothing until he met Raza, bragging how he tortures kerrish. The thief befriended him, but learned little more. They returned to his lodging, and when Raza fall under spell of man-beer, Ya'ousa's thief search his room. All he found was map. He bring map to Ya'ousa, but it useless. Mine is marked but no scale, no orientation." He unrolled a ragged, brown parchment scrawled in black indistinguishable scribing. "With Raza dead, Ya'ousa now give up hope. He must return to home, to Margolyn."

Vareena pushed the enormous paw aside, surprised at the softness of the fur and squinted at the map.

Ya'ousa's bony snout jerked turned towards the tent's opening. He sniffed the air. "Many men come."

A twig snapped in the distance, voices murmured. A shout, and the tramp of many feet filled the hillside.

"Seems men will not leave Ya'ousa alone. Seems Scowl has another chance to prove friendship and trust."

Vareena's eyes widened in sudden discovery, her finger resting at a strange mark upon the map. "Cowl, I—"

A flaming brand exploded in the tent's entrance.

DEATH IN THE NIGHT

YA'OUSA JUMPED backwards, eyes bulging. A torch landed on the roof of the tent, another burned at a wall.

Vareena rushed to stamp out the growing blaze. A large brand hit her a glancing blow and rebounded into a pile of weaves. Ya'ousa's furry paw dragged her away from the flames.

"Come out, Kretch!" an angry voice screamed, while others jeered. "You're going to pay for what you did to Raza!"

Within the passing of those words, the fire found hold, burning quickly at the cured hides. Flames erupted on either side of Scowl, forcing him away from his companions and escape. Red embers fell around him, framing him in yellow and flickering orange.

Vareena feared he was trapped, but something flashed at his side.

IronScythe.

Did she glow? It was hard to tell amongst the growing conflagration.

Ya'ousa dragged Vareena into the cold night amidst

angry shouts of the men and women who had come together for this burning. The mob boiled with hatred at their appearance. Their detestation echoing in hissing, barking tones.

Trapped inside the scorching leathers, Scowl stood motionless. Somewhere in his lost past those same voices of hate had united in aversion against him. He had nothing but a half-formed memory from childhood, but it was strong enough to fill him with rage.

Raising the She-blade, he stared in confusion at the glowing metal. *The IronLight again? Why?* He slashed through the smouldering leather of the tent wall. A man waited for him, his mouth a leering rictus of hate that turned to horror as his eyes caught Scowl's exposed features. A stifled scream and IronScythe found her mark, planting herself in his throat. Blackbeak twisted her, driving the gurgling, dying man down on his back, grating her against the bones of his neck; letting her relish the death.

Many torches glowed. A huge crowd had come for a kerrish burning. Yet IronScythe had her own particular fire.

A deafening, animalistic roar and, to the left of him, Ya'ousa and Vareena were revealed as figures as if in a dream. The girl struck out with her blade, catching an unwary attacker in the face. He fell forward. She elbowed him in the guts, hacking at his head. He crumpled, blood splashing.

Ya'ousa jumped aloft, spinning high in the air, striking out with his wedge-like lump of fenneral. Smashing arms and legs, crushing shoulders and thighs. And when the men grouped against him, those legs bent again to take him far away from their angry blades.

Scowl had no time for contemplation. Men drew in

on him from all sides. IronScythe flashed and stabbed like lightning from a black whirling cloud. Heads and limbs fell thudding onto the hillside. None could escape the intent of the eldritch blade and its shining, devastating light. Blackbeak stole life from the fallen with murderous grace. A man with a smashed leg put up a defensive arm. IronScythe removed the limb before pinning him to the ground in a quick thrust, silencing his pleading voice forever. A moan to his left, and again the She-scythe struck—vicious and brutal maybe, but superb, wondrous and deadly.

A group of seasoned warriors with tanned skin and swords glistening with cleaning oils, made a stand against him. Even their coordinated efforts could not resist the berserker in their midst. Scowl shrieked and charged. The men stumbled and fell, and he was soon to find his mark.

With their fighters slain, and the bright blade twitching for their doom, the mob panicked and ran. IronScythe was not sated; she craved more blood. She sliced at thighs and necks, ripping through the air to cleave nerve and sinew, muscle and bone. When the hillside was empty, she returned for the wounded. The pleading men's cries only fuelled her efforts, and they too fell into ruin.

Ya'ousa appeared at Blackbeak's shoulder. IronScythe swung at him. The enormous kerrish parried with his club of fenneral. At the touch of the curious white and black stone, the IronLight vanished and Scowl collapsed to his knees exhausted.

For a moment the man-animal stood with his weapon raised in anger, but as his eyes opened to the destruction around him, the rough bludgeon fell to his side.

The tent was nothing more than a few smouldering

rags. Ya'ousa kicked around in the ashes, stooping to pick up a burnt corner of the map, his big mop head falling to his chest. "Gone," he said, letting the singed bit of parchment fall to the ground.

A noble voice rang out behind him. "No Ya'ousa, I can find your mine, I know I can."

"But how, Man-girl?"

Vareena felt sick, was as appalled at her own ability to kill and maim, as she was awe-stricken by the carnage staining the hillside. But that unmistakable feeling of power had engulfed her again, and she was powerless to resist. *Is it something to do with the peculiar light surrounding Scowl's blade or that lump of gold in my pocket?* Dead faces accused her with blankly staring eyes. In a convulsive movement, she grabbed the kerrish and held him tightly. "Let's leave here."

Enormous arms enfolded Vareena.

"Darkness would have been done tonight," Blackbeak said. "But iron is the reward for all those foolish enough to let hatred dominate their lives."

Vareena laughed, high and nervy, mixed in with sobs and hysterical sounds. She never understood his simple justifications. "What was that light surrounding your blade? I have seen you fight before, but you were turned a mad-man."

"The Ironlight," Scowl rasped. "A rare thing, usually. Yet twice, recently, I have suffered its uncommon glow." The close-set uneven eyes stared into Vareena.

"It is not my doing," she said, fingering the lump of gold within her weaves. "Is it?"

"I cannot ignore Fulminara's prediction, nor your destiny."

"What is the IronLight?"

Blackbeak considered her question for a moment,

cleaning IronScythe by stabbing the blood-drenched blade into a snowdrift. "Something invested in iron. I do not know more."

The kerrish bowed. If the exchange had intrigued him, he did not show it. "Again Ya'ousa is in your debt, Scowl. Your trust is more than proved."

"Please, for the sake of the Gyre, let's go," said Vareena with impatience.

Blackbeak studied the smouldering remains of the tent. His hood was gone, burned with everything else.

"Man-girl, you say you can find mine?" growled Ya'ousa, as they hurried into the night.

Vareena was still shaky. "Something hidden in the fold of the map. I glimpsed a drawing."

"Tell Ya'ousa."

"A lith-stone."

"What?"

Scowl pointed his ugly features towards the kerrish and nodded. "The lith-stones belonged to an ancient past before delving, to the Golden Age. Some call them 'Travellers Stones'. Columns of rock, now mostly fallen and left in ruin—their secret is lost upon the cold winds of time, Vareena."

Her head shook with irritation. "For once, you are wrong my friend. If we can find one of these liths, I'm sure I can find the stone marked on the map."

Blackbeak's head twitched, shrugging. "The secret has been lost, it—"

"No Scowl, listen. Below each pinnacle is a squat building—a bolt-hole. A place to hold up against the night and the worst of the weather. Carved on each building is a mark. A symbol that tells you where you are. This sign points to others, and the direction you must take. We need to find one of these liths as a point of reference."

Ya'ousa stopped, one great paw covering his mouth, his gruff voice shaking. "Ya'ousa saw such a stone two days past. Old it was, broken. He seen many on his travels. Tell Ya'ousa secret, he needs to know."

"It's not that easy to explain, nor to understand."

"If at all," interjected Scowl.

"Kerrish try!"

"I once knew the cypher, but it was a long time ago, an idle fancy when I was a child. I'm sure I can work it out if you take me to this lith-stone. What do you say, Scowl?"

Blackbeak snorted, his head shaking in resignation. "Where there is gold, there is always delving. Besides, word of this night will surely pass to other towns, to Palim. And I am—unmistakable. The roads will be watched. We can only expect trouble if we continue. We travel with Ya'ousa."

"Good. We go tomorrow. Under light of sun. Ya'ousa tired. He sleep now." He found a sheltered hollow and fell immediately into slumber.

Vareena and Scowl spent a cold night huddled under gnarled, leafless bushes that provided scant protection from the freezing wind. Tomorrow and the rising Sun was all that mattered.

HARNA

"**HARNA LIKE** sky and trees above, they do not care much for stone," boomed Ya'ousa with pride. They entered a rocky crevice forming a natural hollow in the hillside, magnifying the many grunts and murmurs, the chewing and grinding of flat teeth.

Before them were four creatures of such preposterous design that Vareena's mind could not at first fully comprehend them.

"The kerrish riding beast," said Scowl in explanation. "Harna. I have heard of them, but never seen one with my own eyes."

The animals came alive with hollow hoots and croons. Wide nostrils flared at the end of stunted snouts, long tongues lolled out of peculiar mouths. The largest of the bunch—enormous and bulky, with massive flattened paws covered in dense hair of white and tan set against the black flesh of its muzzle—lurched towards them on strong but cumbersome legs. A low stubby head shook with unrestrained joy. The creature's movement was a mess of unbalance and wasted energy.

This is a riding beast? thought Vareena. *The back legs are too small and squat, compared with the powerful forelimbs twice the length.*

The creature charged and Vareena yelled in alarm. Scowl stumbled backwards, his hand coming to rest upon IronScythe.

"Do not worry," shouted Ya'ousa, a laugh contained somewhere inside his barrel voice. "These beasts not cause hurt. No. This is Taatchi, of the Forest." The beast slid to a sudden stop, splattering the kerrish with mud and grass. Ya'ousa slapped the creature's forehead that sloped backwards to a ridge of pointed bone and guffawed. Taatchi tried to bite him with snapping teeth. "Ygirrit tu ankum, ya ellasteer bak!" chided Ya'ousa in his native tongue, giving Taatchi a wry glance.

The harna murmured in response, lifting his head to examine Ya'ousa's companions.

Vareena glanced at the face and let out a yelp. Taatchi jumped back, nudging closer to his master.

"What is it, Man-girl?"

"The eyes—" She was lost for words. They were large, set far back into the enormous head, protected by many eyelids and flaps. A grey iris surrounded by white. Like—*human eyes.*

"Ah yes. They stare. They study. They have eyes of men! See, are not Ya'ousa's the same?"

Vareena pushed back her lank hair, and studied the kerrish's face. Outlandish. An enormous man-animal, deformed in limb and movement. Fur-covered, wet-nosed and snouted—long, yellow teeth poked from his maw in an attempt at a smile. A horror by any other definition. Yet something special dwelled in his brash expression and intense brown eyes. *But they are the eyes of an animal. Nothing like what I just glimpsed.* She nodded politely.

"We kerrish do not share same origin as harna. No. They much older than us. Wiser. Yet we are like kin."

Taachi spat, and then seemingly chuckled. Ya'ousa laughed also. "Now we choose your rides." The kerrish had changed. His grim personality softening in the presence of these animals.

Vareena's eyebrows leapt upwards. "Rides!" she cried, staring after his enormous back.

Ya'ousa returned with a young sturdy beast three heads taller than Vareena, but younger and smaller than Taatchi who stood with comical authority.

"This is Purl, which means *murmur of hidden forest stream*. He now yours, Man-girl."

"Mine?"

"Gift of harna is sacred thing. He is unridden. Purl yours for life. Tella fuh bontek, ah foh rewk unt pffe sah!"

Vareena stared on dumbfounded. "—What?"

"Ya'ousa says *ride long and ride free*. Is always spoken at the *Giving*."

"How can I thank you?"

"No. Do not thank Ya'ousa, thank Purl. Ya'ousa will now go and choose a mount for your friend. You need be alone for a while. Come Scowl."

They left.

Purl turned away, pretending indifference. His hair, shorter than Taachi's, was silken and striped in bands of dark grey, crested with a black, pleated mane.

Beautiful.

The creature spat. A well-chewed bolus whizzed past her ear. Vareena didn't allow herself to be intimidated. She slapped his flanks as Ya'ousa had done. The harna carried on chewing. She rested her left hand upon his front knee where fur did not grow, unconsciously stroking. Purl hummed, nuzzling. She pinched the loose skin. "You like that, Lad?"

Purl turned to examine her. His eyes were a deep blue, irises surrounded by white. Human eyes trapped within animalistic flesh. They stared into her, measuring, yet Vareena had no desire to turn away. A sound akin to a chuckle reverberated in Purl's mammoth chest. *Is he laughing at me?* His wet nose pushed at her weaves, sniffing—stopping at her gird-belt where the single lump of gold lay hidden. He shook his head, blowing out air with a disapproving hoot, before comically nudging her off-balance. She fell on her backside with a shriek.

Ya'ousa and Scowl returned with another harna. Older than Purl, but not much larger. The harna's short sleek black hair caught the early sun revealing a tight well-honed musculature. A breeze played with its brilliant snow-white mane blowing it across an expansive flank.

"Burrstone!" announced the kerrish with pride.

Scowl stood at Burrstone's side, his warped features inscrutable.

Is Blackbeak incapable of any emotion? Is he not similarly amazed by this kerrish gift?

Vareena found her feet, brushing ice from her weaves. Something about Scowl's harna spoke female. She perceived no sexual difference between such beasts; the dissimilarity radiated from within. "A black beast for the Blackbeak. Nice."

Ya'ousa nodded. "Yes. Good fit." The kerrish put his paws on his hips and stood rock still, only his enormous head moved, sweeping from Vareena to Blackbeak, and back again. "You understand this no simple gift? In return for harna, Ya'ousa demand your help rescue his comrades. Yes?"

The barest of nods from Scowl.

"You put a lot of trust in me," replied Vareena. "What if I can't read the lith-stones? What if—"

Ya'ousa raised a dismissive paw. "You help Ya'ousa or not?"

"I will do my best."

"Good. Now we start. There no trick to riding. Is easy. One lesson is all. Harna enjoy carrying you, they love burden. Kerrish not ride otherwise. It help, however, to be confident. To think what you do at all times," he said, pointing at his head, a stubby claw showing them the importance of the information his words could not properly convey.

They nodded.

"You only need learn not to fall off."

"Fall off?"

"This first lesson, Man-girl. Listen. One day you fall. Like season of the Gyre, it will come! If you ready, you not much hurt, yes? But riding easy part. True nature of riding is *look-after* of animal. Harna need care, attention." His bullhead jerked towards four sturdy saddles protected from the weather by a rocky overhang. The largest was more ornate, the wood stained black and decorated with intricate beadings matching the beads upon Ya'ousa's weavery. The seats held many pockets and bags from which brushes and combs protruded.

Ya'ousa then spoke about feed, exercise, tack upkeep and clothing. They listened, repeating his words while fixing ropes, reins and saddles. He checked their harna, adjusted straps and ties, and led them away.

Although nervous about the lesson, Vareena was full of pride as they left the rocky hollow, pleased at the new way Ya'ousa treated her. *To think only yesterday, the kerrish race was unknown to me. Creatures of a childish nightmare. Ya'ousa is nothing like the Kretch I know so well.*

An enormous paw reached down to her leggings and tugged. "Too tight. Leg weaves must be loose. Is same for you Scowl-man. Material gathers at knee and rub. No good. Change soon, yes?"

They walked for an hour westwards, skirting the broken land of the Grikes, and came upon a small twisted forest bordering a low plain. Most trees had lost their covering of green, although isolated saplings, hungry for the sun's rays, still kept their yellowing leaves.

Vareena was keen to get in the saddle, though nervy. Scowl remained distant, unmoved.

"We learn to ride now." Ya'ousa led their mounts around in a tight circle while they studied the harna's untidy bounce and outlandish movement. "Only in speed do they become Margolyn's greatest gift," he said, as much to the vast vault of the sky as to the two novices.

The harna behaved in an almost sarcastic, superior, way—as if they were in touch with a greater world of which Vareena knew nothing. It made her want to ride even more, to prove she could master them. *And yet, for all their muscle and bone, for all their constrained power, they are clumsy creatures.* Awkwardness dominated their form. They struggled against their own muscles and weight like the cumbersome strongmen of her dead uncle's court. The stubby back legs lurched and staggered, occasionally tripping and snagging each other. *How can any rider stay aloft on such a beast?*

Then came the time to mount. Scowl jumped up in a single bound. Confident and relaxed, a smirk crossing his ruined features.

Vareena placed her foot in the extra leathern

stirrup used for mounting. The mountain of flesh rose impossibly high above her. "I can't," she blurted.

"You mount," said Ya'ousa. "He ready."

"I'm not sure I—"

"You mount. Purl yours now. Remember, he sturdy, but is uncomfortable for him if you not mount with care. Watch. Grab mounting pommel here, take weight on right arm, see? Try to avoid your weight dragging saddle towards you. If you mount bad, harna expel air and is chance saddle will slip. Look out for this."

"I don't think I can reach."

"He not bend for you. If cannot climb up like Ya'ousa show you, then get helper. Always mount easy. But Man-girl not need helper, Vareena big enough without."

Scowl turned away, his smirk turning into a smile.

He's loving this. But, if he can do it, so can I. And following Ya'ousa's simple reassuring directions, she pulled herself clumsily into the saddle—and nearly slid off the other side.

Ya'ousa adjusted the stirrups for her leg length, and against her earlier assumption, the saddle felt secure.

The kerrish was last to mount, his steed grunting with sudden effort. Up to now, the harna hadn't moved. When Ya'ousa gave the command to trot, the world jolted and jumped like the shaking lands common to the season of Blaze. Vareena forgot all his instruction. She pulled on the reins in panic. Purl's nose lifted and he came to a halt.

Ya'ousa chuckled. "Riding is always shock, but true grace comes from speed. We go faster soon. First, we try again."

Vareena clicked her tongue.

Purl, pricking his flat, comical ears, lunged forward. The peculiar gait of the harna thrust her backwards, then forwards and, as if this was not enough, flung her up and down. Vareena clung on for dear life. *No one can ride like this. It is too uncomfortable, I'll throw up my breakfast if we don't stop soon.*

Ya'ousa motioned to go faster.

Vareena wasn't sure she could take much more, but at the barest flick on the reins, Purl doubled his speed, and with speed came a new fluidity. Vareena was no longer thrown this way and that.

"How is it?" shouted Ya'ousa.

"Good," answered Scowl.

"Faster?"

"Yes, let's go!" Vareena whipped the reins and Purl hooted in response. She darted past Blackbeak in a rush of pounding paws and flying snow. She glanced backwards. Burrstone was matching Purl paw for paw. Gone was clumsiness. In its place: a lithe, effortless bounce. *Purl is holding back, he is capable of much, much more.*

Burrstone trumpeted with pleasure.

Vareena's thighs began to ache. She clung on too tightly. "I'm sorry, Boy," she said, relaxing. Purl responded and, for the barest of moments, she received the strangest sensation—a four-footed impression of security, as if she understood what it was like to be Purl, to be harna. He monitored each little jolt of speed, silently asking Vareena if he was going too fast or too hard for her. How he communicated such thoughts, she could not fathom, but Vareena felt protected, perched as she was, upon the massive, racing animal.

Scowl, riding astride Burrstone, thumped past, his beast's paws showering her in snow and ice. A silent urging from Purl and—the race was on.

"Faster!" she squealed, releasing all control to her

animal.

They charged across the powdery snow, the acceleration flinging Vareena back against the raised saddle. They raced neck and neck, until, with a subtle understanding, the pace dropped and they came to a shuddering, jolting stop.

Ya'ousa rode up to them. "Always," he said, with a rough approximation of a smile, "they take to it as if they were born for it! But remember, is not rider who important but harna under you. Without him, you could not ride like wind. You both need practise. Never should harna adjust to you, but you to him. They struggled with you. Always *listen*. Harna speak to you in thought and feeling, a feeling you can trust forever."

"Thank you, Jantiff Ya'ousa," said Vareena, tears in her eyes.

"Hah! The greatest of gifts, perhaps, bar one, and only *Thank you?* Yet Ya'ousa understand. It feels right. It feels good. We not go too fast now. Harna prefer speed—they like the wind in their hair and can travel vast distances in great hurry—but must start slow always. Find rhythm, then comes speed. And Arn is a smaller place."

He spoke again. They listened to his words, corrected their posture, concentrated and thought; and rode again.

There was no need for reins this time as both harna responded to their silent urging in an exultant burst of speed that took them past Ya'ousa and his harsh laughter, and hurtled them towards their goal.

LITHS

THE FIRST sight of the lith-stone lying in ruin around this little hillock, thrilled Vareena. A growing excitement gave her a sensation of invulnerability. She leapt off Purl and ran towards the lichen-stained boulders of deep black, veined with a pale limning of blue. Beauty still lived within this tumble of fractured, jutting stones and low stumps. The once-majestic pinnacle had fallen long ago. Only its cracked, flattened bottom was visible from beneath mud and vegetation— like a giant's foot had toppled the column and smashed it into the ground.

The base building, nothing more than three immense blocks topped by a flat slab roof, stood awry, as if the same giant had attempted to push it over. The structure was broken, riven by the intense seasons of the Gyre and split by its own weight. One wall lurched free of the others, lying at an angle and although covered in mud, moss and yellowy lichen, Vareena spied an array of eroded glyphs and symbols. Yes, she thought. The vague outlines made sense to her mind. *I can use this as a sentinel. A starting point.*

"Be careful, Man-girl!"

Vareena ignored the kerrish. *All I need is a dagger or poniard, a wet rag and—*

A huge hill-boar charged from its lair close to the fallen column. Vareena tried to dodge and took a glancing blow, falling onto her back. The black-haired, squat razorback squealed in anger. Twin tusks jutted from the feral-pig's lower-jaw like two scythes; it twisted, preparing to charge again.

Scowl raised his poniard of iron in his half-hand and readied to throw. A furry paw knocked the wicked dagger from his grasp. Blackbeak glared at the kerrish with confusion, his other hand finding IronScythe. "What are you doing?"

Ya'ousa's answer was to toss back his grey-furred head. A bizarre sound, like a soothing roar, escaped from his throat; a weird, animalistic cant. Behind him, Burrstone, Purl, Taatchi and the other harna added to this threnody. Each produced a peculiar un-Arnish lament. A harmony not of two notes, or three or even four, but many.

The hog slid to a stop, black ears twitching. Its dreadful tusks were only inches away from the bemused face of Vareena.

A discordant tune reminiscent of old forests and silent, imposing trees filled the air. The harna sang what sounded like an ancient lament—*a warning*. The pig snorted, beady eyes turned towards the riding beasts in confusion. Hot breath escaped from a flat snout in twin fogs of frosty air. The song changed, became gentler. The boar's breathing slowed and, with a defiant snuffle, the creature retreated backwards to its hole.

A bark from Ya'ousa, and the refrain ended. Vareena reeled, grasping for a balance she already had.

"Ya'ousa is sorry, Scowl." Intent brown eyes fixed upon the poniard lying on the ground. "Is not kerrish way to kill, unless unavoidable."

"Never touch my iron again!" Blackbeak rasped, dismounting and landing in a crouch. He grabbed at the dagger, holding the grey blade close to his chest, his gloved half-hand curling protectively around the curved hilt. Burrstone was agitated, as if she shared his anger. At the touch of his iron, his mood softened. He stood up. "But it is not my wish to kill when unnecessary."

"Ya'ousa react without thought, is Jantiff, is high in Cland. Is difficult for him to change ways of lifetime."

"The matter is at rest."

Ya'ousa nodded respectfully, flinging himself off his harna and approaching Vareena. "Is safe now. Silly razorback will stay in hole. Will not come out." He lifted Vareena up with a strong arm.

"What was that song?" she asked, staring in awe at the harna. They seemed pleased with themselves, chomping on bits of exposed green with loud, snapping teeth.

The kerrish shrugged, enormous shoulders rising and falling like twin slabs of furred rock. "Is nothing. Kerrish know razorback not want to attack. He late to sleep, getting ready for cold season, warm in his hole. We are in his territory, and he must defend. Harna warn him. Tell him he cannot win fight."

As if in reply, Taatchi lifted her flattened head and hooted into the sky.

"Ya'ousa's homeland of Skourass has many such animals," he explained. "We call him *razorback, the angry pig*. He always quick to rage. Dangerous. He not ask questions! He can kill with those hasty tusks of his. Hah! Even kerrish jump up tree when he come. Then we kerrish respect him even more." Ya'ousa chuckled.

Vareena raised her eyebrows. "Thank you again."

Scowl pushed past her, walking towards the lichen-covered stone. He cleared away the congealed vegetation and muck, using his poniard with precision.

She had not seen the blade in full sunlight. A wicked thing of grey twisted metal. The dagger appeared warped, bent as if by tremendous heat. She shuddered.

Blackbeak revealed a series of complicated filigrees underneath the yellowed lichen, the iron scraping and scratching.

When he was done, Vareena pushed him aside and fingered the eroded grooves. *The code I learned as a child, but no secret to the ancients who created this signpost.*

"Well?" said Ya'ousa, unable to contain himself.

A crack in the clouds, and sunlight framed Vareena in gold. "Give me a few minutes to make sense of this."

Ya'ousa turned away, frustration showing in the creasing of his snout.

Blackbeak put a calming hand on the kerrish's shoulder. "Do not hope too much. These stones are old and Vareena—very young."

"Shush!" said Vareena. "If you can't say anything positive, don't speak at all."

"Come," said Ya'ousa, walking Scowl over to where the Burrstone stood. "Let me tell you about Margolyn's greatest gift. About our harna."

Blackbeak rubbed his half-hand down Burrstone's tightly packed black hair. Unlike any other creature, the harna did not shrink in fear or revulsion at his presence or touch. Instead, she hummed with content.

"Harna come from the forest, from Margolyn. Do not worry, Scowl. They untouched by shadow. They exist before the arrival of kerrish and will exist long after our departure. Ya'ousa could spend many days in story of harna, many months on our entwined history. Is their joy to ride. We cannot force them. So was falsehood in part, to say, Ya'ousa give harna as gift, for they only lend themselves. They will be yours for all life if you want, but still only *lent*. You understand?"

Scowl took a deep breath, letting it escape from his ruined nose with a familiar rasp. "I can sense delving, Ya'ousa," he said as if admitting a deep, dark secret. "I can sniff out its illness wherever it may lie. I am made for such things. That is my purpose and yet, if there is an opposite feeling to such ugly rancour, to such woeful evil, it is invested in these creatures."

The kerrish's snout parted, the skin pulling back to reveal an array of yellowed teeth. "Yes, Ya'ousa understands," he said. "We kerrish would be nothing without harna. Nothing."

Taatchi crooned. One big foot kicked at the wet snow, showering them both in slush.

Blackbeak shook ice from his mane-like flock of black hair. "Ya'ousa, you say you are a Jantiff in Cland Totu?"

Ya'ousa's chest expanded like a furry balloon. A raised paw thumped against his magnificent weavery and a roughly hewn badge. A circle of wood rudely painted with reds and blacks. "This Ya'ousa's Mark. Mark of the Totu Cland."

"From what I know of the Margolyn, and its Clands, it is not common for kerrish to travel alone, especially those of rank. You are far away from home my friend."

The huge bullhead searched the empty sky. "We kerrish sometimes too proud, Scowl. Clandsfighters sometimes too hard." He looked down at his distorted, ruined limbs. "We are an afflicted race, are like twisted tree in forest—it lives, but we know the wood inside is rotten."

"You have not answered."

The man-animal scowled. "Ya'ousa travels alone on a noble errand. That is all you need to know." He turned away. The furry back hiding the quick show of emotion incongruous with anything Scowl had heard about the Clands.

Vareena's noble tones broke into the silence. "—We are to the northwest of Palim and directly south of the lith-stone marked on your map. Well, at least, that's what I think."

"Man-girl has solved puzzle of ancient stones?" Ya'ousa blurted with a joyous growl.

"Took me a bit of working out, but yes."

"How long to travel there?"

"We must carry on northwards for at least a week, till we find your lith-stone. Then a short day's walk northeast to the mine.

Ya'ousa pointed a claw at her. "On harna or foot?"

"Of course, Purl. I forgot we were riding. I've no idea how fast and far these harna can travel. We will be crossing *The Grikes*. I'm sure the broken land will be just as treacherous for harna as ourselves."

"Man-girl may reason that, but Ya'ousa know better. Harna travel faster and farther than you think. If you have no goal, harna like you—slow, aimless. Give harna purpose and she like dart on wind!"

Four days later, they arrived at the lith of their destination, facing north above a long, winding ravine atop a tall, craggy hill. The land had become a bleaker place, pocked and chiselled as if some preternatural hand had twisted immense swathes of rock into weather-beaten pedestals. Once gentle rivers and streams had created a riven landscape of deep meandering valleys, sunken holes and convoluted watery caverns.

"Mining Country," whispered Scowl.

Ya'ousa shivered.

The lith-stone had somehow resisted all that the Gyre had thrown at it. It stood high and proud, buttressed underneath was a similar squat building of black slabs. Here grew more exotic, yellowy lichen—the glyphs highlighted as if by gold.

The journey had passed with little incident. Vareena had attempted to explain how the stones worked. They existed in repeating patterns that, once understood, would spread out like an array in front of your eyes. The knowledge was an idle fancy of her youth and, like such things learned in childhood, it had stuck in her mind.

Scowl gave up trying to understand this impossible feat of memory. Ya'ousa had been more than intrigued. During the three nights of encampment, he swallowed all that Vareena could teach him on the subject.

The kerrish thirst for learning was well known. It worried humankind who feared such deformed creatures and envied their riding beasts. There was flesh to their concern: the kerrish organised themselves into socio-military groupings. The Clands. A dangerous force if united in war. They were tolerated by Cairn and the Usery, a protection that many despised.

"Something wrong here," blurted Ya'ousa. "Lith-stone unbroken, Gyre has not eroded. Is unnatural."

"Yes," answered Scowl. "Delving."

Vareena's head jerked towards her two companions. She did not share their sense of doom. Instead, she thrilled with a growing excitement. *The lith-stone is a beautiful thing, magnificent.* "We must follow the ravine north-eastwards."

The kerrish raised a fur-covered arm and pointed in that direction with a rough claw. "Look!"

Low on the horizon rose oily smoke.

"Mines," said Blackbeak.

The kerrish lowered his arm and pondered. "Ya'ousa thinks we must leave harna hidden. He does not like it here. Harna feel it too. We take them to safe place. Then we go."

Scowl nodded, and Burrstone grunted her approval.

Ya'ousa produced a small pouch of red powder and another of blue, white, yellow and black. He then searched for five flat stones. Using a trickle of water from his leathern flask, he mixed these powders into a collection of bright paints.

Vareena and Scowl looked on with a certain understanding. Taatchi was painted, as was the fourth harna. Purl and Burrstone carried only the badge of the Totu Cland.

"Here. You must mark your harna. It is way of kerrish, of harna-lore. You must put your sign upon them."

"But what'll I paint?" said Vareena.

"Think of home," answered Ya'ousa. "Think of your life. You will find your mark."

"My home is Keep Krall. I'm not sure I'll ever return there. It has bad memories for me," she said. "But long before I entered its walls, my father gave me a ring. It bore the seal of Krall. A hunting bird, a flying predator of blue-black wings, bright eyes and a noble, if not dangerous, aspect. That will be my mark, Ya'ousa." Whilst she spoke, Vareena painted the magnificent bird upon Purl's flanks. The curious harna looked on, twisting his flattened head and nodding as if in approval.

"Man-girl paint well," grunted Ya'ousa.

"Before I discovered the sword, I was a master with the brush and the needle." Vareena's free hand patted the hilt of Scowlsbane. "Of course, I must include this," she added with a smile, grabbing at the white paint, daubing quickly, but with precision, "to remind me of the nemesis of delving's gift."

"The white sword and the blackened bird," said Scowl, and upon his lips those words contained a hint of darkness.

"Is good," said Ya'ousa as Purl crooned in delight. "And you, Scowl-man? What is your mark?"

Blackbeak stood transfixed. He could not think of anything he belonged to. No order and no creed—nothing in his past from which to create a symbol.

Vareena saw his concern, and without thinking, grabbed his half-hand and plunged it into the red paint and onto the black flank of Burrstone. The mark, half a palm with stunted fingers and thumb somehow fitted. "Now you have a new name: *The half-hand.*"

Scowl said nothing, only stooping to clean the crimson from his fingers. If he approved, Vareena could not tell.

The three adventurers found a secluded corral where bits of green poked through snow, and left their harna to graze.

"They wait here for us," said Ya'ousa.

"And—and what if we don't return," asked Vareena, suddenly worried she would never see Purl again.

"Harna go home. Back to forest. Back to Margolyn." He patted Taatchi.

The kerrish's expressions and moods were hard to read, but Vareena was sure he shared her apprehension.

A short while later, they entered the valley on foot. Vareena fingered her lump of gold, her pace quickening, anxious for her companions to hurry.

"We will arrive soon enough, girl," said Scowl.

Vareena did not hear him.

Delvers

Scowl sniffed at the oily water gurgling over a rocky streambed, letting his fingers play in the stunted flow—evidence of a fenneral quarry close by. Mining of all types disturbed him. Removal of stone caused no permanent harm to the land but the smokes and slicks reminded him of ages past when gold, silvers and irons were the reef exploited by diggers and tunnelers.

He sighed. IronScythe was also the work of delving. She was an unavoidable evil—to destroy the wicked, you sometimes needed a weapon of equal malevolence. *Will I ever be free of her?* The question often came to his mind. She had been lost to him time and time again, but the cruel iron always found a way back to his hand.

"You in pain, Scowl-man?" asked Ya'ousa standing at his shoulder. Vareena walked a hundred or so feet ahead out of earshot.

Blackbeak stood to his full height. "Of a sort." A laugh like a hiss, escaped his lips, his hand coming to rest on the long hilt of his blade.

"Ya'ousa is aware of how such banes are not all

evil, nor have heinous purpose. But Ya'ousa has seen IronScythe at work. She worries him. How did you come by such a sword?"

"That is a question for another time. For now, she is your ally. Be thankful. You do not want to become her enemy."

"You threaten Ya'ousa?"

"No, my friend. I speak fact—that is all. To carry such a bane is a burden indeed."

The kerrish pondered those words for a second or two. "You wish for something more?"

"What I wish for is irrelevant. I am bound to the She-blade's iron. Without her, I am nothing. With her, I can at least have half a life."

"Then Ya'ousa understand."

"Do you?"

"Kerrish live only half-life too. We not long-lived like man. Kerrish span short. We suffer disease and infirmity and live in fear of what we call the *long-death*. This is why kerrish fight one another. Why Clands always fighting. Better to die quick."

"I have heard of this," said Scowl. "To gain in rank, you must slay your superior in combat. You are Jantiff. Many you have killed to get to where you are, and even more who challenged you for your status."

"Scowl speaks truth. Kerrish take life day by day. None trust to live to sunset. No feelings for kerrish. No true friendship, just words. No love."

"From what I can tell, there is little hope in your race—other than to die in combat. And yet you and your brethren are far from your forest home. You have abandoned your Cland, despite how proudly you wear the Totu badge. I have also heard of others—outcasts from Margolyn roaming the lands."

"Ya'ousa no outcast! Margolyn is his home. Always."

"But why then did you leave?"

"Harna."

Scowl pondered his answer for a second. "Go on."

"Time with harna changes kerrish," he began. "Ya'ousa not like any other of his race. His span is nearly two passings of the Gyre. Ya'ousa is older than any other kerrish who has ever lived."

Blackbeak's misshapen face showed shock. "Two passings of the Gyre—you're no older than a teenager. Even Vareena is your elder."

"'Tis true."

"I knew you were short-lived, but this is a revelation."

"Yet Ya'ousa is old. Is *oldest*. That is why they let him leave. And over his many seasons, Taatchi of the forest has been with him, has shown him new way to be. Ya'ousa believe harna try to heal him, to heal all kerrish—to fix us."

"I don't understand."

"Taatchi helped Ya'ousa to—" the voice faltered, turning into a low growl "—Taatchi helped Ya'ousa not be afraid."

"From what I know of the Clands, they are fearless."

"No, Scowl, they frightened of everything except death. Death is their only friend. Their only certainty. The kerrish are afraid to live." The kerrish thumped a heavy paw into Scowl's back, a growling laugh erupting from his furred maw. "No. Harna have changed Ya'ousa. He mended. Harna will also mend Scowl-man."

"That I very much doubt," said Blackbeak. "Come. There is delving in these hills. I can feel its ugly call."

They caught up with Vareena, and stole silently up the steep-sided valley, travelling through winding gullies worn smooth by the regular passing of feet until they reached a wide bowl. The rocks here were cracked, a vast area of opencast mining. At its centre stood a high-walled compound from which came the sound of water and the voices of men.

At a signal from Ya'ousa, they clambered up the valley wall and lay prone, looking down into the quarry and its compound. An ice-laden waterfall splashed into a large artificial pool. An eddying mist hugged the ground through which walked ghost-like figures.

"About thirty to forty men," said Scowl

"Thirty-eight," grunted the kerrish.

Blackbeak twitched his head. "And more we cannot see, I'd guess."

"Many swords shine. They not made for tunnelling or digging. Weapon-men."

"You are right, my friend."

"Something wrong here, Scowl-man. Man has fenneral mines in our northern land, but not like this. See high compound wall?"

"You reckon that's to keep people in?" said Vareena.

"Not people. Kerrish slaves."

Wet fenneral rested in glistening heaps in the centre of the compound. "Two mine entrances," said Scowl. "They dig underground."

"It looks like a normal stone mine to me," said Vareena. "Fires used to heat the rock and a pool of water released in sudden deluge to quickly cool it, causing fractures and—"

A man ran out of the smaller mine entrance, shouting. More men followed him. Yells and screams stabbed up to their hiding place. A flurry of panic filled the compound below.

Two dust-covered animals also emerged from the mine—slow, encumbered by rocks attached to ropes tied to their feet.

The earth shook, followed a second later by a deafening boom. Black smoke, flames, and a hail of debris erupted from the tunnel, engulfing the two animals.

"Nhulya!" Ya'ousa shouted, jumping to his feet, his voice swallowed by the echoes of the explosion ricocheting around the rocky quarry. It took all Scowl's strength to pull the kerrish back down.

Long moments passed as the dust settled. The two animal captives stirred, stumbling amongst the rubble. Ya'ousa breathed a sigh of relief. "She alive," he rasped. "Nhulya is alive."

Vareena looked on with entranced eyes. She had expected Ya'ousa's brethren to resemble him, to show some kinship in form and shape. Only two things were the same—their obvious animalistic origins and an over-powering deformity. One creature had a distortion down the right side of its body, as if an artist, unhappy at his painting, had tipped water down half its length and the colours had run into each other. Its good side was muscled and sure. Dust-covered brown fur framed a long-snout from which canine teeth protruded and a pink tongue lolled. A withered arm was strapped to its side, a leg bent and twisted. "Marks of delving passed down to punish the innocent," said Vareena in a whisper.

"Watch your words, girl, have you learned nothing?" chided Scowl.

But Ya'ousa was not listening, his full attention was on the scene below.

Scowl pointed his misshapen face at Vareena. "The Bacchust Isle taught me things you cannot begin to comprehend. Yet no learning can match the confrontation of evil. The feel of it down your spine, the insidious cold crawling around in your sensibilities. You know of what I speak. You were with me in the lair of the golem. Such evil comes with rancour. A smell like old sweat on a summer's day. Yes, the origin of the kerrish is shrouded in perversity, but delving and dark majiks do not taint their souls. They rose above their beginnings. Became something else. Something good and noble."

The cloud of smoke settled to reveal the second kerrish. Grey with black dust-stained patches, a thick tail trailed behind a squat body. A man dressed in the manner of Raza and those who frequented the tavern in Fisk, went up to them and started shouting.

Ya'ousa grumbled to himself in his own language—a fearful sound.

Scowl sniffed the air. "They are using powders. No wonder they keep their mine secret."

Vareena took a deep breath. "Powders?"

"Yes, evil things, fulminating tinctures used for display and exhibition, turned to volcano-flame by desire for metal. This is no fenneral mine, despite the show. I can smell their delving."

"Ya'ousa feared as much. Since Nhulya disappeared, he has heard rumour of such thing, but could not believe it. Is Scowl sure?"

From one of the low buildings, a round figure emerged. He was covered head to foot in yellow.

"By the Smokes!"

"That's—that's gold," whispered Vareena. There was something almost delicious about the display.

Scowl unsheathed IronScythe in a single convulsive movement, as if the presence of gold alone was enough to set her free.

Vareena was familiar with the She-blade. A shadowy, blurred thing. Yet she couldn't face her in the full glare of sunlight. Contained in the iron was the same metal that glinted in the sun before them, a thin limning of gold. The heinous arts of delving rested in IronScythe. She seemed too much for one person to control. There was no envy, no greed for such a weapon.

"Is gold dangerous to you?" asked Vareena.

Scowl's head shook side to side. "No, Vareena. The threat of gold comes from Chicanery. You must never touch, nor go near such metal."

"You can't tell me what I can and can't do. You're not my master."

Blackbeak's eyes remained fixed upon the glinting golden god that lumbered towards the kerrish captives. "If it is your destiny to take up the majiks, you cannot have anything to do with such metal. It will corrupt you, change you—it will burn a black mark across your soul. But there is another danger. The Great Age of Darkness was the result of the delving of the land. Its metals should remain buried."

The kerrish thrust his bull-head towards Vareena. "Man-girl possess majiks?"

"It has been foretold, Ya'ousa. She will become She-savant. Although she must conquer her arrogance before that can become a reality."

Vareena turned away. *What does he know about my destiny? Scowl is jealous.* She squeezed at the nugget of gold in her weaves. *It's as precious and as necessary to me as Scowl's iron is to him.*

Below them, the gold-arrayed figure stopped in front of the two man-animals. In one deft stroke, a golden weapon flashed and removed the head of the grey, squat-looking kerrish. It raised a second time.

"Nhulya!" bellowed Ya'ousa, jumping up and brandishing his club of fenneral. His animalistic voice echoing from the sharp walls.

The golden figure turned towards the powerful sound. The other men looked up also.

Before Scowl could stop him, Ya'ousa bounded down the side of the hollow.

He moved with incredible speed, jumping and skipping in a sideways gait making the best of his deformity. He leapt from rock to rock, swinging his club of fenneral in front of him. It was a feat of physical power and precision incongruous with what appeared to be his major weakness. Ya'ousa reached the compound wall and leapt, landing badly atop the rough barricade. He wobbled for a second and fell. The men ran forward, and the kerrish was lost amidst many bodies.

"We have to help him!"

"We cannot," Scowl rasped. "Ya'ousa did what he had to do to try and save his mate. He does not expect us to sacrifice ourselves also."

Vareena's emerald eyes flashed with anger and confusion. "But we can't do nothing!"

Scowl's head shook. "It is not my way to sit idly by, but not even IronScythe can win-out against so many. She will not willingly let herself fall into the dominion of delving and gold."

Fists rained down upon the kerrish. A sword-hilt to the head, and Ya'ousa dropped for the last time. Nhulya, struggled to get to him, but she too fell under the force of many blows. At the direction of the figure dressed in gold, two rough looking men dragged the kerrish away, a thick line of blood curled in the dust behind Ya'ousa's limp frame.

"Thank the Gyre!" Vareena whispered. "They did not kill him. We can try a rescue." She turned her eyes towards Scowl. "Can't we—?"

A sound like a sigh escaped Blackbeak's lips. "This is a gold mine, Vareena. It must be destroyed. If we can save Ya'ousa while doing that, then yes. We will try."

"But how? We are just two, and they are many. Do you have a plan?"

Scowl ignored her urgent questions. "Some of those men have the look of Arakian mercenaries from south of the Ingram Sea," he said with a scowl.

"Arakia? Is that important."

"My travels once took me close to that land. It is a stain polluting the South. I have heard many rumours that delving still lurks there, but iron drew me north, to the Unbidden Isles and Oldiva. But when her attention again turns to the South, they will come to feel the cold edge of her blade." Sweat dripped from his brow. Scowl's face had taken a haunted look.

"Are you all right?"

"'Tis the presence of so much delving metals. Of this little golden god. We must beware. *You* must beware."

A shadow passed over Vareena's face. "What'll we do now?"

"We wait till dark, and try to find a way inside."

"Dark? Use your eyes. There's no way in, other than through the front gates. We've not the legs of Ya'ousa."

"Time and iron will show us the way."

Vareena drew breath to reply, but the compound's massive gates were suddenly thrown open. Many men poured out, running towards their hiding place.

They scrambled backwards out of sight and dropped down into the ravine, running. The gully became alive with men.

Vareena and Scowl had little cover among the rocks. She took the lead, moving with strange purpose. A rock formation ahead caught her attention. It seemed familiar. She ran towards it, finding a tight gap. She squeezed through, followed by Scowl, and emerged into a small hollow dominated by a giant bramble.

Scowl's uneven iron-blue eyes furrowed. "You've led us to a dead end."

"No, look." She pushed the bramble aside to reveal a boulder-strewn hole.

The sounds of men echoed from behind the gap.

"Quickly!" Vareena jumped into the hole, swiftly followed by Scowl. They landed a few feet down in the dark. A second later, two men pushed themselves into the hollow above. They muttered for a few moments, and left.

"Here." Scowl handed Vareena a dried stranding taken from his pack. With a whisper from his misshapen lips, it burst into life.

They stood in a man-made cave. Roughly circular with twin ruts in the floor. Dripping walls lent the tunnel a fetid air. The end had partially collapsed, creating the hole they had escaped into.

"We are in an old mine," said Scowl. "We must be careful."

Vareena shivered, but not from the cold. She was filled with excitement. "I think this tunnel will take us to their mine.

"How can you be so sure?"

"I don't know. Just a feeling. I have led us well so far, have I not?"

Scowl bent his misshapen features to the darkness ahead and sniffed. He was reminded of Fulminara's prophesy. Yet the caves of Vareena's doom were many leagues and seasons away. "Are you sure?"

The torch reflected in her eyes, flickering across the glassy black of her huge, excited pupils. She seemed powerful, arcane. "Let me lead you, Blackbeak. I'll find a way."

CALL OF THE CAVES

BLACKBEAK SNIFFED at the fusty mine air and extinguished Vareena's stranding with the thumb and forefinger of his stunted half-hand. "Gas."

Vareena was surprised by a low-level light that seemed to emanate from the walls.

"Bad gas down here. We cannot use a torch, nor breathe too deeply." He pointed to the tunnel walls. "I have seen this light-bearing lichen before. It grows in foul air. We must be careful."

They had descended into the abandoned mine workings for over two hours. Vareena led them with a sense of purpose. If this worried Scowl, he did not show it. He followed one step behind, silent except for the wet rasp of his breath.

Occasional sounds leaked from the surrounding rocks. Creaks and moans like the far off groans of trapped men. Vareena knew of the shades that inhabited dark, damp places. Of the direful voices that tried to trap the curious and the foolish. "Do you believe in ghosts?" she asked.

"Don't waste your breath on such silly questions."

"You do not believe in the shades of dead men. Of all those killed working in this mine? Trapped here. Forced to roam these tunnels forever?"

"They bother me not. Only the real world is worth any thought or curiosity."

"You are not frightened that they may try to lure us into traps and dangers?"

"You breathe too deeply of the gas, Vareena. Miners also hold the same superstitions. No dead hand can harm that which is living. Fear them not. What is dead is passed, what is passed has left forever."

She found strength in his matter-of-fact dismissal, but the groans did not go away, if anything, they became more human, more woeful.

At the next juncture, Vareena felt the breath of cleaner air coming from above. And slowly, they ascended, leaving the under-mine behind. Her pace quickened and soon, the faraway thud and scrape of digging, of mining and the real world, replaced the groans of ghosts and shades.

"I'm impressed," said Scowl. "Although I'm intrigued by how you managed to guide us so well?"

"I don't know. Maybe it's something to do with Fulminara's prophesy. Maybe it's my—it sounds odd to say this, but it could be my majiks again, helping us, helping Ya'ousa."

"I hope it is just that, and not the lure of gold. You must keep away from it. The metal can harm you irreversibly."

"But does not gold sit in your She-blade?"

"IronScythe is designed to combat delving. She cannot affect you, be sure of that."

"But what if I know gold can do me no harm."

"You cannot have such knowledge."

She reached into her weaves and pulled out the ingot of gold Raza had used to impress her. "It fell from his hand when I killed him. I couldn't leave it behind."

A flash of horror crossed Blackbeak's misshapen features, replaced by fierce anger. "You little fool!" he barked. "Now I see what has pushed you upon this journey, what has pulled you into this mine of delvers. You needed no lith-stone to guide you here. Rid yourself of it, now! Before it is too late."

"You're not my master. You can't tell me what to do!"

"Do not dare to disobey the will of iron, Vareena. You do not know the danger you are in."

"You can't lecture me. Your precious weapon is also made of forbidden metals, of iron and gold. Will you not also throw her away?" she spat. "Or does the *Hooded Scourge* live by different rules?"

"You speak of my iron? You are not fit to be in her presence." He unsheathed the She-blade and raised her with threat.

Vareena took a step back. "You don't scare me. I know when and where I will die."

"Have you not listened to all I have told you since we met? Iron is the nemesis of delving, *of delvers*. Of those who seek power from dark majiks. You risk her fury!"

"You threaten me?"

"Not I, but IronScythe."

"But you control her?"

"No, Vareena, I but carry out her will. You must throw away the yellow metal or feel her wrath." He pointed his blade at Vareena's face.

She stood firm. "Have you forgotten Fulminara so quickly? Her words. You cannot kill me, Scowl."

"No?" He swung IronScythe around his head,

the blade keening and worrying in the dark, wafting Vareena's lank hair.

She was defiant, unafraid. "Iron is not my master and never will be."

He stepped forward, knocking her to the ground. "That is gold speaking. And you are foolish to trust the Carline."

"Am I?" she said, raising herself upon her elbows. "If I had not helped you, you both would be lost. Fulminara's reward was given in good faith. Deep down, you know that."

Scowl's head twisted from side to side, a desperate look in his eyes. "IronScythe's power lies beyond the fate of any one person, Vareena. She can break prophesy and destroy oracles. No one is safe from her. Do you not yet understand?" He raised the She-blade above his head.

Vareena baulked. "Don't!"

The sword came down, plunging deep into the rock floor only inches from her head. He let go of the blade and fell back into the gloom.

Long moments passed as she lay under that dark metal, her heart beating in a flurry. When she again found her feet, what met her eyes filled her with dismay. Scowl lay upon the tunnel floor. A twisted ruin of a man. *Without his blade he is nothing. The She-blade wanted my blood. Yet he stopped her.* Guilt overtook her then. Distraught, she looked at the nugget of gold in her hand and for the first time found evil in its appearance. Like some dreadful golden watching eye. She threw it down the tunnel as far as she could and went to tend to her friend.

"I'm sorry, Scowl," she said, staring at his warped physique. An awful malaise inhabited his limbs, some constricting force twisting his legs and arms, hands and feet. He shook and quivered as if in apoplexy. *More animal than man. The creature I first saw in King-Emperor Jhaz'Elrad's Reeving Chamber.* "Forgive me."

Blackbeak did not answer, weakened without the touch of his iron.

Guiding his one good hand to the hilt of IronScythe, Vareena gave him back his dignity.

At the touch of the grey metal, Blackbeak breathed deeply, taking strength and power from the iron. His limbs relaxed and straightened. But it was long minutes before he was strong enough to speak.

"Gold," he rasped. "Gold does this. We are both its victims." He stood up, wrenching IronScythe free from the rock floor, showering the pair of them in rocks and debris.

Vareena jumped away from the rubble, her eyes staring at the wavering tip of the now free blade. IronScythe trembled for a few minutes, hanging in the air close to her face.

Warning me.

Finally, Blackbeak sheathed the blade. "You have been lucky. It is not many that IronScythe has spared. She lives for punishment, for vengeance. Sometimes even the innocent are not safe.

"I did not realise, Scowl. Truly."

"Gold is the curse of Chicanery. It is through this metal, and through irons and tins, that the majiks flow. A sacred part of the earth. Once removed, it can push any savant, regardless of his or her good character, into insanity and hate. You must be careful, Vareena. This is a gold mine. You stand amongst its reef."

"I've felt different ever since I took the nugget from Raza. I heard your warnings, but—"

Blackbeak grabbed at her weaves with his stunted half-hand. He pulled her close to him, face to face. "You forced yourself upon my company when I did not want it. You ignored my advice at every opportunity. After we rescue Ya'ousa and I destroy this mine, I want you gone. Do you hear me? IronScythe perverts those around her. All fall to her blade—if you stay with me, she will one day take your life. And I will not be able to prevent it."

"It's a chance I'm willing to take." Vareena leaned in and kissed his exposed cheek. It was unplanned, and yet it felt natural.

Scowl reacted like he had been stung, pushing her away. "Come, there are more important matters ahead of us. Let us concentrate upon our task and nothing else."

Vareena followed him. "What did you mean earlier, by 'destroy this mine'?"

Scowl said nothing, but Vareena didn't hold out much hope for the delvers and their pits. *As for Scowl?— He cannot get rid of me so easily.*

GOD OF GOLD

THEY HOLED up inside a smaller ventilation tunnel close to the now-abandoned lesser mine's entrance. The thin, cruel speech of the southern men echoed around them. They hissed and whispered in a peculiar cant that expressed moods and understandings in staccato repetition and long drawls. It rose to an echoing crescendo with the rough shout of many gruff voices and sank to a menacing jeer that crawled around their hiding place.

Even Scowl seemed bowed under its cadence, his warped face occasionally grimacing.

Vareena thought she might go mad with its sound. "Why do they do it?"

"You ask me this? You have already felt the pull of gold upon your mind."

"But—"

"Listen Vareena. Chicanery, like any other Crafting, has its shining lights and its disappointments. Some savants can evocate with the power of ten lesser users combined, while others only gently caress their majiks.

And there are many who will never have the ability to take up the azure-robes, but within whom the majiks still flow—even if that flow is but a trickle."

"You mean—?"

"Yes, it seems that this Jessop is drawn to gold by his own majiks, however small the flame burns within his breast. And for some the pull of gold is irresistible. It gives the owner natural authority, charisma. It gains them acolytes and blind followers. Henchmen. With gold, Jessop can experience real power."

"You're saying Jessop is a savant?"

"A part of Chicanery? No. He is no more dangerous than the next man. You know the type—a philanderer, a man of easy words and easier pleasures. The weak-minded are drawn to him like flies to ordure. He is apt to inspire loyalty in his followers. A big fish in a small, murky pond. But with gold in his hands? It is like a magnifying glass, making him more than he is. It would seem that this Jessop represents the force behind this mine, and behind the use of kerrish slaves. It is likely that he and his men are getting rich from gold-trade with the South."

"But he must know of the risks he is taking. He must realise what he's doing?"

"He is an addict, Vareena, as are the others. Gold is a drug many find hard to resist. But worry not, they will all be punished. Now be quiet. We must wait till nightfall."

The sounds of men digging and toiling stretched over the long hours until the short night finally fell and the men downed their tools. Scowl lit a torch. "Now we search," he said, his nose sniffing at the gloom.

"Search?"

"Yes, for the miners' delving dust, their powders."

"But what about the men? We cannot wander their mine at will, we will be discovered."

"You forget, Vareena. Miners, especially delvers, are superstitious. They leave their workings under darkness for fear of the dead. Of ghosts and shades. No, we will be quite safe."

"But should we not go find Ya'ousa? He is in danger."

"I have but one task now that I know these men are delvers—to destroy them and their mine."

"You can't forget the kerrish. The gifts he made to us, your vow to him. You can't."

"I have not forgotten, but if we are to rescue our comrade, we will need a diversion."

"But—"

"Silence! I seek to kill two crows with one fire-hot stone. If Ya'ousa still lives, what we now do will be his only chance."

Vareena sighed in resignation. "Come then, let us be quick."

They ran, navigating their way through the mine's many levels, softly padding through well-used, winding tunnels until they neared the other, larger entrance. Scowl extinguished his torch, for the tunnels flickered with candle light and strandings. They revealed abstract paintings, weird carvings, and the bleach-white of whittled bones. Here and there were alcoves in which rested the rotting remains of food offerings and the occasional sacrifice. Scribbled parchments, blotted and stained with dry blood were pinned to the walls. The whole mine was a shrine to sickness and death.

Scowl stopped, his misshapen nose twitching. To their left was a small opening. He entered a dry, gloomy cave, pungent with the smell of sulphur and the bitter taint of urine. Here, covered with rough weave sheets, was a stack of roughly hewn barrels. "Good," he whispered in the dark.

"Have you found it?" asked Vareena, following him, carrying a lit stranding taken from the wall outside.

"Stay away," he barked. "One ember from that torch and both our futures end here."

She stepped back into the entrance.

Scowl broke open a small barrel with a quick thrust and twist of his poniard. A muslin bag rested inside. Unravelling the loose knot, he revealed the dark powders. "We shall use their delving ways against them."

"But what of Ya'ousa and his mate? Night is short. They may already be dead."

"Ya'ousa accepted his fate. He knew what he was doing," said Scowl. Stuffing the bag into his gird-belt. "Now extinguish that flame and help me."

"I'm not like you, Scowl. I cannot be so cold. I need to see if they are still alive."

"It will achieve nothing. You will endanger yourself."

"But I must. And besides, my end is far away in another time and another land, I will be safe."

"Such knowledge is already making you rash and over-confident, Vareena. You must watch those emotions for one day they may be your undoing. Fulminara only prophesied when and where you will die. Forty-three passings of the Gyre is long enough to suffer much injury, loss and pain. When your end comes, you may wish it had come sooner."

Vareena digested his words. "Only Scowl could turn such news to darkness and woe. I'll be careful. Now get on with your work."

A sound, like that of a hissing toad escaped his uneven lips. "Try and find where they are keeping Ya'ousa and Nhulya prisoner, but do not attempt to talk or get close to them. Understand?"

"I won't get caught. Will you be alright on your own?"

"Remember the gas?" he said, expertly rolling one of the barrels.

Vareena nodded.

"It mixes well with delving powders, and they have quite a store. Be careful, Vareena."

"I will." She left Scowl to his plans and stole towards the mine entrance.

A massive fire burned in the centre of the compound, roaring into the black of a starry, cloudless night. Golden motes, like a swarm of fireflies, flew into the sky. Many men surrounded the fire, dancing and gyrating, drunk on beer or some other substance.

A ceremony or a sacrifice?

A flash of gold and Vareena almost cried out. Standing directly behind the pyre, catching glints from the flame that burned orange and incarnadine, was Jessop.

Rings, bracelets, necklaces, and amulets; heavy pieces of flattened and worked gold covered his neck and arms. He wore a belt of gold upon which hung a great golden sword. The yellowed metal had been fashioned by reverent hands, scored and filigreed by skilled, although misguided, fingers. The hilt was a claw encircling a golden globe: a crude representation of the planet Arn.

The symbol of his authority. A beautiful thing, but IronScythe she is not, thought Vareena.

Thick flesh slid over the gold of many rings, making it difficult for Jessop to bend his fingers. Gold entwined his head like a crawling snake. It banded his calves, and pierced his ears, nose and belly. It adorned all visible parts of his body, dancing hypnotically in the light from the fire: a liquid demon of delving.

Vareena felt dizzy. *Scowl's words make sense now. I can feel Jessop's gold. It wants me to take it, to own it. I won't let myself get tempted again…* But she could not take her eyes away.

Sometime later, how long she knew not, a commotion outside a row of squat open buildings like cowsheds broke her reverie. Vareena shook her head, coming back to herself. A group of men stumbled towards the pyre, dragging the two kerrish captives between them. Both Ya'ousa and Nhulya stared ahead, ignoring the scene around them. *Scowl was right. They have made their peace with death. It does not scare them. But they may not have to die. Not if Scowl can pull off his plan.*

Blackbeak arrived at her side. "The fuses are lit, the mine will blow soon," he said. "How fares Ya'ousa and his mate?"

Vareena nodded towards the two bound kerrish, made to kneel before Jessop and the pyre.

"Superstitious fools." He spat. "The land is not appeased by such sacrifice. Bones can never replace the loss of gold. A burning will not free them of their crimes. But do not worry, we may still have time to save them." Iron-blue eyes roamed the compound. "There are fewer guards than earlier, but the gates are still watched. Come."

They crept out from the mine entrance, hugging the auburn-tinted shadows. On the other side of the fire, many men sat cross-legged in a roped off area.

"Prisoners," Vareena whispered. "They may aid us."

"No."

"How can you be so sure?"

"We can trust no one in this den of delving."

They stole further into the orange night, moving from rubble to building.

Jessop's rounded belly jutted fatly from beneath his chest-plate, emphasising his stubby legs. Red-faced and ill looking, his eyes yellowed and red around the edges, he wheezed and spluttered unhealthily. He smiled at the prisoners, revealing even more gold: a ring in his upper lip.

Scowl pointed towards the prisoners. "Look Vareena, they too have such a ring. A sign of Jessop's dominion. And his snare. The pull of yellow metal traps them; they would rather die than live away from its allure. We can trust no one to help us."

Vareena was reminded of the curious hole in Raza's lip. Fisk, and its little tavern, seemed a long way away from this perverse scene.

Ya'ousa and Nhulya were kicked to the ground. And, as if this was a sign, Jessop began to speak.

"We hass come long ways my frens, travelled far northes from our lands. We hass come great distances cross kingdoms an' seas for tha feel of hot gold upon our hanss. Toiled an' fought, dug an' delved."

The followers of gold moaned and groaned in recognition of these phrases. They drank heavily, as if the ale contained opiates.

But Vareena now realised what really befuddled their sensibilities: *gold*.

Jessop continued. "But tonight, let uss gives a little back tah tha land, for she's `ungry an' needs her bones returned. Bones!"

Vareena was almost mesmerised by the voice. There was something uncouth about the accent of Arakia. It had no tongue of its own, but spoke the common language with a twisting lilt that slanted words. A compliment in that land sounded like a sugary insult.

They scrambled closer to where Ya'ousa and Nhulya lay.

"An' nows—nows is tha time for tha payment tah be made!" Jessop lifted up his golden sword and muttered, half to himself, half to the crowd. *"Give her bones— Bones—Bones!"*

"Where is your diversion?" whispered Vareena.

Scowl glanced back to the mine entrance. "Curse the works of delving!" he hissed through uneven, clenched teeth.

The golden god's face turned to one of hate. He took a step toward the kerrish captives and spat at them. "You whose were created by delving, shall dies forrit!"

Scowl's powerful, yet nasal voice reverberated from the gloom. "Jessop!" It was as if the land itself had found vent for its hatred.

Blackbeak entered the cauldron of flickering light and unsheathed IronScythe. He walked with slow purpose, raising the blade before him.

Frightened, thinking their master had summoned some dark creature of delving, the men pulled back from his path.

"Whose—whose are ya?" demanded Jessop.

"I am the avenger of darkness and delving. I have come to claim what is mine."

The light of the fire caught Scowl's blackened and ill-wrought nose, the smashed ruin of his face and the intense unblinking iron-blue eyes. It cast unnatural shadows upon his face—as if some preternatural heat had melted his features. His blade crawled and danced.

Jessop nearly fell over backwards at the sight, his befuddled followers wailing in a chorus of fear. The grip upon Ya'ousa and Nhulya was loosened. Vareena noticed they were tensed, ready.

"Gets back! I am gold!" shouted Jessop. "Duzzent let him fools ya! He's nah avenger of delving, he's an ugly friend of tha Kretch!"

The men murmured in confusion, but a few reached for their weapons.

Scowl chose his moment well. He held up IronScythe threateningly. "You think gold is power? I challenge you to put it in contest against the power of iron!"

The earth grumbled and shook, roaring from deep within its depths. A series of conflagrations exploded from the mine entrance, sending Jessop and his followers, scurrying away from Scowl and his dark weapon. Stone missiles riddled the air, smashing into rock, wood and flesh. Fire erupted from sudden cracks that opened in the ground, incinerating men where they sat and catching others as they ran. Human torches staggered and stumbled, screaming in terror and pain.

Ya'ousa and Nhulya jumped to their feet and, although tied with thick ropes, they used the sudden commotion to head-butt and bite their captors. Blackbeak and Vareena ran towards them, bringing twin blades of stone and iron down to slice their bonds. The dazed men were easy fare—IronScythe butchered them into so many cuts of meat.

"Run!" Scowl shouted.

The four of them sprinted towards the compound's massive gates looming before them in the deafening, exploding night.

"By the Gyre!" Vareena squealed. "I could not believe my eyes."

"My knowledge of powders is limited only to their use, Vareena," he gasped as they ran. "I had no idea if they would ignite the underground gas—although I hoped for that outcome."

Only two men guarded the gate. This time IronScythe was idle. Nhulya ripped into one while Ya'ousa crushed the other with massive paws. Neither missed a stride.

Then it was IronScythe's turn. She spun in the air and split asunder the great wooden beam that held the gates shut. Pushing with the might of four bodies, they escaped into the dark night.

Once outside they were met by the sound of excited hooting, low bellows and the thick rasping sounds of harna.

"Yak tek fejjik tullo pah buh gragwerren!" growled Ya'ousa angrily. Taatchi pushed his enormous head at him and the kerrish's angry words were soon replaced with those of greeting.

"Purl!" Vareena was pleased beyond belief to find her new friend waiting for her. She mounted easily, keen to leave this place behind. There was no saddle, but contact with Purls thick neck lent a warm feeling of security and reassurance. The earth continued to shake with underground explosions.

Nhulya crooned to her harna who was joyous at her side. Only Burrstone seemed quiet. Scowl stood by her, his half-hand stroking her sleek hair.

"Quickly, Scowl. Mount!" Vareena shouted.

Scowl shook his mop head. "You go ahead. There are things I must do. Wait for me by the lith. I shall return before sunrise. If not, remember me well and look after Burrstone."

Before Vareena could say anything to stop him, he strode through the breached gates and into the compound, Burrstone crooning sorrowfully at his back.

Vareena urged Purl to follow him, but Taatchi blocked her way. "Leave him be, Man-girl," grunted Ya'ousa.

"But he'll be killed."

"Ya'ousa think not."

"But—"

"Did you not hear Scowl speak out against gold?"

"What?"

"He challenged with iron. Such a challenge cannot be left unfulfilled."

Ya'ousa and Nhulya urged their harna forwards. And despite Vareena telling Purl to turn back, he followed them, leaving the gates, explosions and the collapsing compound far behind.

POWDERS

Scowl strode through the gates of the compound. Around him, the vast quarried hollow began to collapse in on itself. Soon there would be no evidence that a mine existed here at all.

He marched forwards, searching for the little god of gold. Confusion reigned as men struggled to escape the still exploding mine. Few noticed the tall, sable-weaved nemesis that stalked the compound, and if they did, they gave a wide berth.

A flash of yellow, and Scowl caught a glimpse of Jessop hiding behind one of the small buildings. He lifted his head and looked straight into Blackbeak's vengeful eyes. Jessop called out to his men in fear, but even his commanding voice was lost to the surrounding din of shouting, and the boom and ring of blasts deep inside the rock. Terror-stricken, the god of gold ran.

Scowl followed, his pace unchanging as he stalked his prey.

Jessop reached the compound wall and turned to face his pursuer.

"I have come to set my iron against your gold, Jessop," said Scowl. "Let's see how your blade fairs!" He swung IronScythe, but despite Jessop's shaking hand, he parried with his golden sword. Scowl was momentarily taken aback. He swung again, and again Jessop blocked his strike.

Something about the gold would not allow IronScythe to pass.

A smile crossed the yellow-bathed features. "Sees? Youss cannot conquer gold. It alone destroys. Youss are no avenger. Irons is no match."

They engaged in a frenzy of attack and defence. Scowl and IronScythe twisted and turned, stabbed and slashed. Blackbeak tried every trick; every move he knew, but could not pass the golden wall that was Jessop's defensive blade. Yet all the power of Jessop's gold could not turn the combat to his advantage.

Blackbeak became aware of a ring of men watching them, drawn to the spectacle—and to the gold,

"Face it, ugly! Youss has lost. Jessop commands all. I say, kills him. Kills him now!"

Another blast from the mine entrance and flaming coals fell around them in a burning hail of fire.

Scowl's grasped for the muslin bag held in his gird-belt and threw the contents at Jessop. Powders clogged the gold, sticking to it with a weird adhesion.

An ember caught Jessop's shoulder and ignited him into living flame. Fire licked at his face, burning his hair and peeling away the skin so that it became one with the melting gold. He fell forward Herd, screaming and shouting. Fat hands tried to stifle the flames. But it was no use. Thick drops of fat bubbled and frothed, guttering down the heated metal—leaving behind a blackened, smoky ruin of melted gold, twisted limbs and charred bone.

Scowl faced the shocked men. "The Land has had her sacrifice." As if in answer to this offering, the earth rumbled, a deep resonating growl that convulsed in paroxysm after paroxysm. Blackbeak was thrown to the ground. Deeper groans followed, the terrain cracked and fire belched.

The valley exploded in a deafening roar that buried it forever.

Arnhenge

THE HARNA crooned sorrowfully in the bright dawn, their haunting sounds reflecting the destruction around them.

A series of rumblings, lasting long into the night, had devastated the land for leagues. When they had reached the lith, it too lay in ruin.

Whatever force has kept this silent sentinel untouched for so long was unable to resist the might unleashed last night, thought Vareena.

If not for the dextrous speed of their harna, they would have been caught in the collapse. Ya'ousa had taken a heavy fall and Purl, too, was hit by a glancing rock, but their desperate gallop rushed them to the farthest reaches of catastrophe, and they had been saved.

"The Land reclaims its own," said Nhulya. Her voice thin and reedy, as if it struggled to pass through her animalistic mouth, but her words were warm and soothing. Her command of the common tongue made Ya'ousa sound like a child. Vareena nodded in understanding.

White mist hugged the ground, gently dissipating upon an early breeze. It was an eerie scene. The sun shone low on the plain, her disk pale and cold.

The landscape had changed forever, becoming a featureless, flattened, rock-strewn wasteland. A whole area of the Grikes had fallen in on itself in a landslide of boulders and stones.

There seemed little hope for Scowl. "Is he dead?" Vareena whispered to Ya'ousa. "Will he return?"

The kerrish breathed in deeply. "Air is fresh this morning, is clean. It speaks of new beginnings. Kerrish have many skills, many powers, yet knowledge of future is unknown to us."

"Then you cannot tell."

"That is not entirely true," said Nhulya. "In return for this shortcoming, the Gyre has given us a heightened ability in the now—in the moment."

Ya'ousa nodded enthusiastically. "Ya'ousa feel that Scowl is not dead."

"But then we must go and look for him."

The kerrish shook his head. "No. We wait."

"But—"

"You have listened to Ya'ousa, but have not heard."

"I can't sit around if he needs our help!" Vareena raced over to Purl, and clambered upon his back. The harna made no response, except to croon sorrowfully. His peculiar face looked up apologetically at her and seemed to frown. "If you won't take me, then I'll go on foot!"

"Stop and listen! …Land is broken. For leagues. Where would Man-girl look? No. We wait. If Scowl survive. He come here, to lith stone."

The words were unbending, but the Kerrish was right. *The Grikes have gone, collapsed in on themselves…*

but I can't do nothing. Vareena dismounted and fell in a heap. Purl nudged against her. She pushed him away.

How much time passed before Burrstone trumpeted at her side, Vareena was not sure. She looked up in a daze.

Scowl's massive black harna raised herself upon sturdy back legs, her head bobbing. She grunted in pleasure; crooning into the thin air of the cold morning, and launched herself across the sharply jutting broken rocks.

Vareena jumped to her feet, searching the mists. A sudden breeze and there he was, standing tall and proud, IronScythe girded at his side. Scowl's weaves were bloodied and torn, but he was alive. Relief washed over her.

Burrstone was first to arrive, nearly knocking him off his feet as she pressed and pushed against him, bathing him in warm blasts of moist air from her widely expanded nostrils—groaning and whimpering and stomping next to him.

Vareena arrived next, jumping down from Purl's back.

Scowl appeared worn thin by the night's events and the slow journey over clint and grike.

Ya'ousa put his paw upon his shoulder and nodded—a sign of deep respect for kerrish. Nhulya too, dropped her head in his direction.

"What happened?" Vareena said.

Blackbeak fell to the ground in a faint.

Vareena was all action. While she tended to his wounds, Ya'ousa and Nhulya lit a fire and heated some water.

A day later, when Scowl had recovered sufficiently, they

made ready to ride.

Vareena was keen to get moving, for she feared the sudden appearance of Bluster, the season of snows and hails, sleets and freezing rains. It was already months overdue. When the snows came proper, it would blizzard for month upon month, covering the land and suffocating the earth. Any unwary traveller could not hope to survive such a time. They needed the safety of a Keep or castle.

The kerrish appeared to be unaware of this danger, and even Purl, her harna, showed a calmness that was against all instinct to the danger that was about to come.

"Ya'ousa senses your worry," said the kerrish, mounting Taatchi. "He sees your fear. But Big-Snow is no threat to us."

"What do you mean?"

"You do not understand about harna. They enjoy snow—love it. On hard ground they are fast, upon snow, they travel lighter, move with greater speed. Blizzard may blind rider, but harna see—they not get lost. If you know where you want to go—harna take you there."

Something in his tone said that this was no idle statement, that the kerrish had a goal in mind. A journey. "I travel to Palimara with Scowl. Will you come with us?"

"Listen Vareena, Ya'ousa is old. Very old. He will never again return his home of Margolyn. He says: let him guide you. Let harna take you South to land of Bikar."

"Bikar? But that's—"

"Yes. Ya'ousa and Nhulya travel to Arnhenge for festival of Alycion. Ya'ousa want to spend his last days in ring of stone. To visit Arn's greatest monument."

"It's an impossible journey, thousands of leagues

away, half the Northern Continent and more."

"Vareena is forgetting harna."

Purl rubbed his snout at her back, nudging her—like he too was pushing her forward upon this expedition.

"But I travel with Scowl, we are—"

Blackbeak raised his gloved half-hand. "Go with them, Vareena."

"But I'm travelling with you to Palimara. To raise an army to… to…" Her voice died.

"You need no Keep, nor revenge. We must part—you know that."

"But—"

The beak-face showed no emotion. "Destiny will find you wherever you are, Vareena. You must prepare yourself for what is to come." Scowl mounted Burrstone. "Goodbye my kerrish friends," he said, bowing to Ya'ousa and Nhulya. "Trust and friendship are never the easiest found, in you are both—with abundance."

"No." Vareena jumped on the back of Purl. "I'm coming with you."

"Goodbye Vareena."

Before Vareena could protest, the harna began to sing. Their multi-tonal voices uniting in a sad lament.

Scowl reined Burrstone. "Look after Vareena well," he said and, with a shout, galloped away.

"Come, Vareena," said Nhulya. "Arnhenge awaits us. Turn your sorrow into purpose. Ride with us. Let Ya'ousa be your guide, and let destiny fuel your actions. Vareena must decide, but follow Scowl-man she must not."

Vareena watched Burrstone gallop into the distance. She could sense Purl. If she so wished, he would follow Scowl. No command from Ya'ousa could prevent that. Yet she had made her decision. *I'm sure we will meet again, one day. I shall look forward to it, my friend, no matter how long it may take.* She allowed her eyes to roam over the land. To the southeast she could feel Cairn, the city of majiks, but was not yet ready to visit its vaulted spires. "Then Arnhenge and the Alycion it is. Let us go, for I tire of this place."

At that, Ya'ousa let out a loud bellow and the three harna leapt away, leaving the ruined lith-stone and the collapsed mining lands of *The Grikes* far behind.

Epilogue: Deluge

A ROUGH hand knocked an elongated pipe from the prone figure's lips. "You wake now!"

The words snaked through Blackbeak's mind. Two men stood above him—the diminutive, wide-toothed hunchback who ran this den of pipes and his enormous gaudily painted servant. Scowl ignored them, reaching for the fallen pipe with a lazy hand.

The old pipe-master kicked it from his reach with a bare foot. "No. You wake. You go. You cannot stay. Wake now!"

Blackbeak raised himself onto one shaky arm. The hyyrh-weed parlour was almost empty. A few men and women lay here and there—like so many corpses. A female attendant flitted between them, stopping only to massage limbs, administer honeyed wine and to refill the long, ebony pipes. She carried a single smouldering stranding—a drunken firefly dancing in slow motion. Roughly drawn erotic pictures hung upon sagging walls. A half-naked Sumac-Priestess lay across from him. She too appeared blurred, a real life hanging of lazy flesh upon tired bones.

"Fill my pipe, or you will feel the touch of vengeful iron," he croaked through a dry mouth. There was no threat in his voice, no anger—the sound was a nasal drone that seemed distant to even his own ears.

Outside the rain pounded, battering against the closed shutters, dripping and guttering in an unremitting torrent.

The pipe-master's eyes dropped to Scowl's side where was strapped the delving blade. It worried the brown-skinned hunchback. "No. You go. You leave." He nodded to his servant.

The bigger man glanced nervously at the forbidden metals. He dragged Blackbeak to a sitting position, buttressing his back with a mouldy bolt-cushion. The pipe-master brought honeyed wine to Scowl's lips. It tasted bittersweet, but was refreshing.

Blackbeak's mind began to clear—images swirling behind the dullness. And pain, like an old remembered enemy, stirred at the back of his mind. "No," he stuttered. "I'm not ready. I need more time."

"No. You bad for business. You must go now. No more pipes. Go!"

Scowl closed his hand around IronScythe's hilt, the touch of the cold metal jerking him back to consciousness. Yet he was still groggy, his limbs cumbersome and listless. His heart thudded as he raised himself onto unsteady legs. "Where am I?"

The pipe-master seemed taken aback. "The finest pipe parlour Caxamaaka can offer," he said with a sneer. "Or was, until you arrive."

"Caxamaaka—the Jungle City?" Memory flooded back to Scowl. He had been in the pipe-parlour for many days—Burrstone would be lonely. *Perhaps it is time to find her and leave this lowly place.*

This excuse of a city with its huddle of poorly built, squat buildings was a haven. Everyone here belonged to the same cruel religion. Sacrifice was common. And ritual. But the city also attracted those seeking the dreamlike escape of the hyyrh-weed. One thing was for certain, since his arrival, he had killed no-one and he and his outlandish riding beast were tolerated. Strangers were welcome here. Mostly.

Scowl grunted. "A skin of wine and I will be on my way."

A few minutes later, he stumbled into a growing dusk, the heavy door of the pipe-parlour banging shut behind him.

This was the season of Deluge, of never-ending storms and the constant battering of hot rain. After the single, bloated sun of Blaze had turned Arn into nothing more than a burnt husk, the rains were soon to follow and with them the first beginnings of the fast vegetation that was already choking these streets in a covering of ever-growing green.

The city was a blurred place, hidden behind the sheen of falling water and a voracious moss that clung to all surfaces like fresh snow. Still, it was a relief to once again see green in place of blackened, scorched earth, even if he was already drenched to the skin. The buildings here were nothing more than rough stones propped together, yet at some time in its past, master-builders had held the sway. The Eastern Pyramid that formed the religious centre of these superstitious people was something beyond the simple architecture now on display—for many weeks now, he had been drawn to the hieroglyph-covered walls. *Maybe IronScythe brought me here to enter its forbidden chambers? Does she not realise*

I tire of combat, of conflict? No, I will find my harna and go.

The joined suns sank in the sky, the heat waning and the rain turning into a steady drizzle. Around him, the night-flowers began to bloom. Tiny pink and blue heads that bobbed in the wet breeze. By morning, they would be gone, but in their place, thousands of pods releasing their spoors to colonise all corners and holes. He had seen this season before, yet always marvelled at this sudden bursting forth of life.

The streets were a treacherous place, moss-covered and slimy, but after a short journey, he approached the building that housed Burrstone. The harna hooted from within, somehow knowing he was nearby. And when he entered, the excitable animal nearly knocked him off his feet. She was a different looking beast to the one he left, her black, elegant fur now coated in green. All animals still awake in this season possessed the same hue. It was impossible to resist the spoors. Only humans, it seemed, were capable of repelling the moss—as if they were not indigenous to this planet. Scowl guessed they were usurpers, somehow arriving from off-world. How they came to be here was as much a mystery to him as his own presence.

Burrstone nuzzled against him. Their connection was not one of words, but of mutual respect. *She is my friend rather than my possession.* As the thought passed his mind, Burrstone crooned loudly, her head bobbing up and down as if in agreement. Harna, *'the greatest gift, bar one'*. Scowl had always understood what Ya'ousa had meant by those words. For him, the greatest gift was an honourable death.

The harna let out a low growl and looked past Scowl to the building's entrance.

Come, Scowl.

Blackbeak nearly fell over. He shook his head. Bracing himself against a moss-covered stone wall. *That voice. It can't be.*

"Yes, Scowl. It is me." The red-haired Carline stepped into the doorway.

"Fulminara!"

"I told you we would meet again."

Burrstone leapt forward, putting herself between Scowl and the witch, sniffing at her.

She stroked the harna's head, with a long-nailed hand. "'Tis a wonder, the harna. You are truly fortunate to own her."

"I am not her master," Scowl barked, unleashing IronScythe.

"Put your iron away. I am not here to fight, but instead to make of you a request."

"I will do nothing for you."

Fulminara shrugged. "This is my favourite season, Scowl. The fertility of the land exploding around us. Does it not startle and amaze you? We Carline thrive in this season. It is a time of beginnings, of new life, of birth."

"Say your piece and be gone."

"I am Fulminara, Queen of the Carline, the last of my kind. It is unfortunate in this season of beginnings that I come to request an end."

"You want me to kill you? That I can accommodate."

The blazing red locks of the Carline shook from side to side. "No, Scowl. My time is nearly over, but I am not fated to die in this land, nor in this season. I speak of another."

Burrstone hooted in derision, as if she sensed the words that were to come.

"Since our last meeting, I have been disturbed. A

niggling worry that has grown over the many months of the Gyre. We Carline can glimpse the *When* and *Where* one may die, but in giving this gift to the girl, Vareena, I sensed something else."

"Go on."

"I have travelled the planes and have found many futures. In nearly all of them, she becomes a Dark Savant. I fear she will bring blackness and death to Arn akin to delving's past. You must stop her, Scowl. Only you and your eldritch blade can intervene with her destiny. You must use your bane to destroy her."

Burrstone's hooting reached a crescendo.

"Did you not hear me, Scowl? Vareena must be killed."

Scowl resheathed IronScythe. "What makes you think I will trust the words of a witch?"

"You believe me, Scowl. Even though you want to pretend otherwise. If you are half the avenger I think you are, you have already sensed something in the girl. She must be stopped."

"Yes, I have sensed something. She is kind-hearted, warm. Headstrong, maybe–but she is young. Vareena will not become this evil you mention."

"Can you be so sure?"

"I would stake my iron upon it." He strode past Fulminara and out into the wet night.

"The fate of many lives rests with you, Scowl. Do not forget that. When the time comes, you must act."

Blackbeak shrugged his shoulders. *It is time to do iron's work. I've had enough of this witch and her doom-ridden prophesies. Let's see what delving lurks within those sloping walls.* He adjusted his grim hood against the rain and strode purposely towards the moss-covered pyramid.

~END~

A Note from the Author

If you loved reading *The Scowl* as much as I did writing it, can I ask you to please leave a review. This is not just for me and other readers, but for a whole host of other boring marketing reasons that I won't go into right now.

Suffice it so say, if you leave me a review on any of the e-book stores, or Goodreads or anywhere else, I'll be *well-chuffed,* and it will certainly increase the likelihood of further novels in this and other series.

Thanks in advance!

K.J.Heritage

Acknowledgements

Thanks for the red-pen, scribbling and 'telling me off in no uncertain terms' talents of my lovely editors:

Dee J. Holmes
Suzanne Buist
Caroline Bean
Blossom Young

Also by *K.J.Heritage*

Mystery and Crime
Dying Is Easy
The Peculiar Case of the Missing Mondrian

Science Fiction
Shattered Helix *(Vatic Book 1)*
Shattered Web *(Vatic Book 2)*
Blue Into The Rip
Quick-Kill & The Galactic Secret Service
The Lady In The Glass - 12 Tales Of Death & Dying

Sci-Fi Compilations
Once Upon A Time In Gravity City
Chronicle Worlds: Legacy Fleet
From The Indie Side

Fantasy
The Scowl

Non-Fiction
All About Copywriting: 55 Easy Edits To Improve Your
Writing Forever
3000 Writing & Plot Prompts A-C: Supercharge Your
Creativity & Improve Your Writing Forever!

Find all ebooks, paperbacks, hardbacks & audiobooks by
K.J.Heritage at the following stores:

*Amazon & Audible, Apple, KOBO, Barnes & Noble/,
Nook, Google, Smashwords & more*

Links

Join K.J.Heritage's *Newsletter*

Get an inside track on all future releases, access to early reading copies (ARCs), sneak previews, and more.
http://kjheritage.com/join

Mastodon

@kjheritage@mastodon.social

Instagram

Photos of my wonderful Shollie rescue #RescueJack, piccies of my best mugs of tea, and various and shameless images of all my books. Oh and maybe yours truly on a good hair day!
https://www.instagram.com/k.j.heritage

Twitter:

90K+ followers
@kjheritage

TikTok

General silliness and book stuff. Search for #kjhtok
https://www.tiktok.com/@k.j.heritage

BookBub:

Not only can you check out the latest cool book deals, but you can also get an alert when I publish my next book
https://www.bookbub.com/authors/k-j-heritage

Goodreads:

Friend me here:
https://www.goodreads.com/kjheritage

K.J.Heritage Facebook Group: *Mostly Readers*
Fun chat and posts about reading… *mostly.*
https://www.facebook.com/groups/mostlyreaders

K.J.Heritage Facebook page
Follow/like and keep in touch with even more writery stuff!
https://www.facebook.com/theauthorkjheritage/

Website:
http://kjheritage.com/

Email:
Want to get in touch? Well here's your chance
contact@kjheritage.com

About *K.J.Heritage*

"K.J.Heritage's uncanny sense of pacing and
story puts him at the forefront of today's
speculative fiction writers."
**Samuel Peralta, Amazon bestselling author
and creator of The Future Chronicles**

K.J.Heritage writes books that he loves to read. From
science fiction action and adventure mysteries to
contemporary thrillers, comedy, and paranormal fantasy.

When he isn't penning third-person descriptions about
himself, he's an international bestselling author writing
the books he likes to read. From psychological thrillers
and mystery sci-fi to crime, action & adventure, and
epic fantasy. He should really stick to one genre, but he's
not that kind of writer... or reader.

His first sci-fi short story, *Escaping The Cradle* was
runner-up in the 2005 Clarke-Bradbury International
Science Fiction Competition.

K.J.Heritage's short story *Churchill's Rock*, part of the
'Chronicle Worlds: Legacy Fleet' anthology, will be
aboard the Astrobotic's Peregrine Lunar Lander set for
launch on the United Launch Alliance's Vulcan Centaur
rocket platform bound for the moon in June 2022.

He has also appeared in several anthologies with such

self-publishing sci-fi luminaries as Hugh Howey and Samuel Peralta.

K.J.Heritage has done all the requisite 'writery' jobs such as driver's mate, factory gateman, barman, labourer, telesales operative, sales assistant, warehouseman, IT contractor, Student Union President, university IT helpdesk guy, British Rail signal software designer, premiership football website designer, gigging musician, company director, graphic designer, stand-up comedian, sound engineer, improv artist, magazine editor and web journo... Although he doesn't like to talk about it. *Mostly. Maybe a little bit.*

He was born in the UK in one of the more interesting previous centuries. Originally from Derbyshire, he now lives in the seaside town of Brighton. He is a tea drinker, avid Twitterer, and neurodiverse (ASD) human being.

FOR ALL media enquiries, event/booking information, signed copies, etc. please email: *contact@kjheritage.com*

All the very best,

K.J.Heritage